REIGN OF MONTGOMERY

Lily Boone

For Mom and Dad.
Thank you for reading thousands of stories to us.
And thank you for listening to all of mine.

CONTENTS

Title Page
Dedication
CHAPTER 1: Montgomery   1
CHAPTER 2: Detrix's Doll   7
CHAPTER 3: The Journey   15
CHAPTER 4: The Knights   22
CHAPTER 5: Luca   27
BACK TO THE CASTLE: PART 1   36
CHAPTER 6: The Nomads   43
CHAPTER 7: Beauty   49
BACK TO THE CASTLE: PART 2   55
CHAPTER 8: Weapons   61
CHAPTER 9: Books   70
BACK TO THE CASTLE: PART 3   76
CHAPTER 10: The Wizard   81
CHAPTER 11: The Creek   88
BACK TO THE CASTLE: PART 4   95
CHAPTER 12: The Ceremony   102
CHAPTER 13: Luca's Squirrel   109
BACK TO THE CASTLE: PART 5   116
CHAPTER 14: Eliza   121

CHAPTER 15: Dreams	127
BACK TO THE CASTLE: PART 6	133
CHAPTER 16: Knighthood	139
CHAPTER 17: Runaway	144
BACK TO THE CASTLE: PART 7	150
CHAPTER 18: Marquise	157
CHAPTER 19: Midnight	163
BACK TO THE CASTLE: PART 8	169
Chapter 20: Knights of Basil	175
BACK AT THE CASTLE: PART 9	181
CHAPTER 21: Memories	186
CHAPTER 22: Plans	193
BACK TO THE CASTLE: PART 10	200
CHAPTER 23: Carac	211
BACK TO THE CASTLE: PART 11	220
CHAPTER 24: Child's Play	228
CHAPTER 25: Hero	237
BACK TO THE CASTLE: PART 12	244
CHAPTER 26: Liars & Manipulators	251
CHAPTER 27: Heaven	258
BACK AT THE CASTLE: PART 13	268
CHAPTER 28: The Sword	275
CHAPTER 29: Reunited	283
BACK TO THE CASTLE: PART 14	290
MARQUISE: PART 1	297
MARQUISE: PART 2	303
BACK AT THE CASTLE: PART 15	311
Felix: PART 1	317

Felix: PART 2	324
BACK TO THE CASTLE: PART 16	331
CHAPTER 30: Royal Engagment	338
CHAPTER 31: Royal Wedding	345
BACK TO THE CASTLE / The End	361
The reign of Lilith (coming Soon)	365
About The Author	367

CHAPTER 1: MONTGOMERY

I looked around the slaves' quarters and saw a shimmering beam of light peering through the cracks. The sun was up.

"The sun is up," I yelled out. I didn't even have time to say good morning to the others. I ran to the castle.

"Why hadn't the rooster crowed?" I thought to myself. But before the thought could even be completed, I looked down to see the rooster's carcass spread across the castle courtyard.

A cat must have gotten him. I picked up the rooster and examined the meat. "Not too bad," I thought to myself. I quickly began removing the feathers from the rooster. This would be what Montgomery ate for breakfast.

I looked up, and Carac was panting, his shirt in his hand.

"Here," I handed him the rooster.

"Why didn't you wake me up this morning, Lilith?" Asked Carac

I rolled my eyes and pointed at the bird. "The cat got him last night. A dead rooster can't crow. I did yell out, as I ran out the door," I explained.

Carac sighed.

He pulled his blond hair back with a strip of material he had scavenged from somewhere. He stood taller than I. Carac had piercing blue eyes I could lose myself in. It hurt me to see his strong hands plucking a rooster. His talents were wasted here as a slave. He could read. None of the other slaves could, and I found that so intriguing about him. He told me he had been stolen from his family by the King and brought here to the castle.

"Frog is waiting," said Carac, and pointed to the castle.

"Right," I said and began running again. That's what we called the queen because she resembled one. I didn't know who had started it, but it was quite funny.

I flew up the steps in the castle and then ran to Montgomery's bedroom. I had to stop before I opened the door to catch my breath. Once my breathing had returned to normal, I carefully cracked the door.

Frog was asleep. Thank goodness. I sighed in relief. If she knew what a late start we were getting, she would have punished me for sure. She would have taken my food for the next 3 days or taken Carac's. Sometimes she would make us watch her eat till she was sick just to prove her power over us.

Life had not always been like this. I had always been a servant but never a slave. I lived next to the kitchen my entire life. I cooked and cleaned for the royal family. I was not royalty by any stretch, but my life was comfortable. I recalled being a child and playing with Montgomery, as equals. When we were small children, we were sometimes mistaken for sisters. We both had long flowing dark hair. The only thing that truly stood us apart was her green eyes and my grey eyes. She had forgotten all of this the day her father died, fighting off attackers to the Kingdom. Felix was not perfect. Felix had captured slaves. Felix had killed men just because they crossed him the wrong way, but Felix had always taken care of me, and without him, I worried about my life. It had been a year since I had seen him. I missed him dearly.

"Montgomery, my dearest queen, morning has come," I said in the gentlest voice I could muster.

Montgomery was draped in pillows and blankets so high that I could barely see her in bed. They were made of white silk, but the color had been so tarnished that they were beige at the absolute best.

I saw her moving, and then the smell began to come from the bed. With every movement, a foul odor emanated from her body. I almost gagged. I had to stop myself. I tried to put my hand over my nose, but I couldn't let her see.

"Slave girl," she said.

She had recently begun calling us slaves, and then our general physical description. That had to be more complicated than just calling us by our names, I thought to myself.

"Get my red wig ready," She shouted.

I went over to her bookcase of wigs. I found the red wig perched on the top shelf. I climbed the bookcase and brought it down to her.

She was standing naked when I reached the floor. She was tall. Taller than most men. I could see rashes that covered her body from refusing to wash herself. She used to have long black hair like mine, but she had cut it short close to her scalp to wear wigs. Somehow, even with her hair short, it stayed matted to the top of her head. It was rare that I couldn't see an insect running through it like a forest.

Montgomery sat on a stool for me to place the wig. I grabbed a jar of pig fat on my way over to her. I put the wig on the floor, opened the jar of fat, and dug my fingers into the jar, then smeared it across her head. This was to keep the wig in place. Once I had finished, I put the jar down and fixed the wig on her head. I looked at the red hair and wondered where it had come from. Or better yet, *who* had it come from. I handed Frog a mirror so that she could examine her own hair. She looked at her reflection and smiled to herself. She reached out and touched the mirror gently, as if greeting a friend.

"Girl Slave, dress me," She commanded.

I picked up the dress she wore the day before and began slipping her arms into the sleeves. The garment was too tight and clung to her sides, but she liked it. It was pink with stains from food across the front.

"Tell the boy slave I would like him to serve me now," she said.

I bowed my head, exited the room, and ran to the kitchen. I found Carac frying the rooster.

"Frog wants you," I said, and grabbed the pan from him so I could finish it.

"Tell her I'm dead," he said without looking up.

I sighed. "You have to hurry," I said.

"Why?" He asked. "Life here is not worth living,"

I took his chin in my hand. "We have each other," I said and tried to smile.

He rolled his eyes. "If I weren't taken from my family, I would be married to a beautiful girl my father had chosen for me right now, you have lived here your entire life, you're used to the life of serving people, I am not." He said.

5

Somehow, his words could cut me worse than Frog's. "You have to hurry," I said as I looked down at the rooster.

He groaned and began slowly walking to Montgomery.

CHAPTER 2: DETRIX'S DOLL

I awoke before anyone else. The owls and crickets were still singing their songs into the night. I gently reached out and touched Carac's arm to wake him. He smiled and rubbed his eyes.

"Good morning," He mouthed to me.

I kissed his forehead.

He leaned up and stretched his arms wide. "Want to hear a

story?" He asked as he reached for his book.

I nodded.

He opened the book, and I could hear the soft paper brush against his rough fingertips.

"Where did we leave off the last time?" He asked.

"I think we were in the middle of the story," I replied.

He nodded. "Right"

While he was reading, I watched him turn the pages and listened to his voice. I sometimes forgot all about the story when I was listening to him. I often spent this time daydreaming about what my life would be like away from this place.

"Do you think you could teach me to read?" I asked.

"Why do you want to learn to read when I could read to you?" Asked Carac

"Maybe I could read the book to you. Wouldn't that be fun? I asked cheerfully.

"Adults can't learn to read. You don't even know how to spell your name. It's just too late for you to learn. You might have been able to learn when you were younger, but it's harder for girls to learn anyway." Said Carac

"The queen's mother used to read to me when I was little," I said.

"She was royalty," Carac snapped back.

I nodded and looked away, fighting off tears. I didn't want to let him know how badly he had hurt my feelings, because if I admitted his words had hurt me, it would anger him further and make him think I was being ridiculous.

I looked at the door and saw the sun beginning to come up. "Looks like it's time for us to get started."

Carac sighed. "Let me finish this story first."

"You know we can't keep Frog waiting. We got incredibly lucky yesterday."

He threw down the book in frustration and walked out of the room. I picked up our blankets and book and placed them back into the corner. If Montgomery found out I had stolen a book from the royal library, she would be furious, even though she found reading boring.

I walked to the barn where the animals were kept. I needed eggs for Montgomery. Upon entering the barn, I was greeted by Wilbur waving. He was both the stableman and a slave to the royal family. He oversaw all the animals. He had a medium build and had grey hair with flakes of dark black hair peeking through. Felix had taken him to the castle as a slave when they were both young men. Wilbur was mild-mannered and had answers for most questions you asked him. He was upbeat and always encouraged me to look on the bright side. I couldn't help but wonder what he was like before he was a slave. I had heard whispers around the castle that he was a knight from another land, but when I finally asked him about it, he just patted me on my shoulder and told me not to get lost in anyone's past. Once I caught him practicing fencing in the barn with a broomstick. I couldn't help but wonder.

"I couldn't help but hear Carac this morning," said Wilbur.

I was startled and dropped an egg on the ground that I had just picked up out of the coop. "Carac didn't mean the things he was saying," I said quickly and went back to putting the eggs in a basket.

"I didn't hear what he said. I just heard him stomping around again. I know you both have something for each other, and he shouldn't treat you like that." Said Wilbur as he took a brush over one of the stallion's coats.

"It's harder for him than for me. I've always been here." I said.

"That's ridiculous," Wilbur said.

I put a couple more eggs in the basket, thinking about what Wilbur had just said. "It's just us three now. I can't afford for him to be even more upset with me." I said.

Wilbur muttered something under his breath in frustration. "You don't deserve to be here," he said quietly.

"None of us do," I snapped back, defensively.

"You are special. Carac has no idea how good he has it here," said Wilbur. "Carac would be lucky to even speak to you if we weren't stuck here."

"Just don't let him treat you poorly. Okay?" Wilbur had stopped brushing the horses and was looking at me like he was waiting for a response.

"I'll try, but you know how hard that can be with his temper," I said.

Carac walked into the barn. "Frog wants you," He muttered.

Wilbur looked at me, letting me know this conversation wasn't over.

I handed the basket of eggs to Carac and started walking out of the barn. Carac grabbed my arm before I could walk out and pulled my ear close to his mouth. "Hey, sorry about earlier. Meet me in our spot in the orchard tonight."

I nodded, but I was still mad at him, and he didn't even ask me if I wanted to meet him there tonight. He just told me.

I walked up the long steps to the castle, and each one made my stomach lurch just thinking about Montgomery. I was pleasantly surprised when I opened the door to the castle and was greeted by Detrix. He was smiling. When I looked at him, I could see a little bit of his father, Felix, in him, although I knew Felix hated how much his son looked like him. Detrix was unlike anyone I had ever met. He was kind, gentle, and had a heart of gold. But Detrix's mind never seemed to grow up like Montgomery's and mine had. He still played with toys and ideas about the world that were childlike in nature. Sometimes this was good and sometimes bad. He often got taken advantage of by his older sister. Detrix stood tall and broad like Felix, and his deep brown curly hair curled around his face. Detrix was younger than Montgomery and me by a few years.

"Lilith!" Detrix shouted and threw his arms around me. "I miss you not sleeping in the castle." He said.

I patted his shoulder. "Don't worry. I'm not too far away," I tried to say with a happy tone, but seeing him sad made my heart hurt.

He quickly let go of me and smiled again. "I have something to show you!"

He pulled one of his dolls from the large pocket of his satchel. "Look! I gave her hair," he said, proudly.

"Detrix, where did you get that hair?" I asked, but I already dreaded the answer, because I knew.

I examined the doll, which had previously been made with a simple glass head and a body crafted from scraps of leftover material.

I heard Montgomery let out a shriek of horror. I handed Detrix back his doll and ran to her bedroom.

When I opened the door, she was holding her favorite brown wig in her hand, but it was missing the entire back of her hair.

"What happened to my wig?" She screamed.

"Maybe the mice got to it," I said. But, as the words left my lips, I felt regret. Even a simple fool could see the blunt marks from a blade.

Montgomery threw it down and looked at me. "You know what happened! Now tell me," She exclaimed.

Before I could open my mouth, Detrix came bursting into the room. "Look what I did," he said, and handed the doll to his sister.

Montgomery stared at the doll in her hands, and her face grew redder with every moment that passed. She took the head of the doll and clenched it in her fist until it burst into a million pieces on the floor. Blood dripped from her palm, but if she felt any pain, she didn't show it.

Detrix was dumbfounded for a moment and then began crying uncontrollably. "My doll," he said through tears.

"You're a man, Detrix! You don't even need things like that anymore. Grow up!" Montgomery shouted.

She stood up and looked at Detrix. "You will be punished for what you did to my things."

I dropped to my knees and grasped my hair, showing Montgomery. "Montgomery, please cut my hair to replace your wig. It's long and it would be enough. Just leave Detrix alone."

Montgomery slowly turned and looked down at me. "Why would I want hair ridden with the dirt of a slave? I would rather cut the hair from mules than wear your hair on my head."

"Guards!" She screamed.

A few guardsmen instantly appeared in the doorway.

"Lilith belongs to the guards now. Please take her out of my sight."

CHAPTER 3: THE JOURNEY

"After years upon years of looking at your cursed face, I will finally be rid of you. My foolish late father's charity will be gone from my sight," she said with a smirk.

My stomach sank.

"You, Lilith, will now belong to the guardsmen. A little reward for them if you will. You will no longer be staying with your 'friends,' Carac and Wilbur. You will be doomed to a life of serving the guardsmen. You will stay in their quarters, never seeing the light of the sun. Obeying even their sickest wishes," She let out a cackle of a laugh. She reached out and grabbed my jaw with her hand and gave it a shake.

The guards came and grabbed both my arms and began dragging me back to their lair. One of them grasped and smelled my hair, while the other grabbed me around my waist so I couldn't escape.

"Wait!," I screamed. The guards stopped momentarily. "My dearest queen, I have an offer you absolutely cannot refuse!" I blurted out.

Montgomery motioned for the guards to put me back on the ground.

"Let me go out into the Kingdom and find the most strapping man in all the lands and bring him back to you. A man to help you make an heir to the throne. A man you would be proud to have by your side. A man who would bring a strong seed. Then, you can do whatever you want with me." I said, quickly.

This was a hazardous job. Going out into the Kingdom alone could be a death wish. There were nomads, barbarians, wild animals, and anything else you could think of. There had even been rumors of dragons by the pirates that sailed around the oceans.

Montgomery paced in a circle. "Slave, you have given me a very intriguing offer, but you must think I am a fool to think that I would just let go out into the Kingdom to run away."

I thought for a second. The guards grabbed my arms and began to carry me. They reminded me of hungry dogs.

"Then, put a bounty on my head no one could refuse if I am not back here in 2 months! Five sacks of grain! The people of Utuk can't refuse that offer." I was hoping that maybe if I found Frog a husband, she would have mercy on my soul and let me stay with the other slaves when I returned.

Montgomery, once again, motioned for the guards to halt. I could hear an audible sigh from both.

"Slave girl... You are a woman; I assume you have desires,..." she trailed off. "...I don't want a man to pick my husband for me. A man would pick a man that had rough hands and a face that scratched my cheeks when he kissed my face." She brought her fingers to her jaw softly, like she was imagining this man. "Maybe this would be in my favor..." she trailed off, talking to herself quietly.

The thought of Montgomery kissing anyone with that foul breath made me sick.

"Fine, release her." Now go, slave girl, you have your orders," Shouted Montgomery.

"Yes, majesty, I will go," I said with a bow.

"Girl, you will need to fetch a horse for your journey. Take Felix's." Montgomery ordered.

I felt appreciated for the briefest of seconds. For a moment, I

17

didn't see the queen. I saw my childhood playmate. The girl I shared everything with, and then Montgomery corrected herself, "Slave Girl...Did you think that was for your comfort? The horse is for you to get there quicker. Don't forget your place. Please find me a husband. You have 2 months, and if you do not return, I will hang your friend Wilbur from the gallows... Now go! Send the slave boy over as you leave."

"Yes, My Queen," I said, a lump in my throat forming. This was not the deal I wanted to make.

I quickly exited. "How am I supposed to find someone else's husband in 2 months? That was the most ridiculous offer I had ever made." I thought to myself.

I ran to the stables. Wilbur was still brushing the horses.

"Wilbur, I've made a mistake," I said, crying. "I need a horse. Right now, I must find a husband for Frog."

Wilbur pulled out a stool and motioned for me to sit. I finally caught my breath to speak.

"I have promised Frog I will find her a husband in 2 months. If I'm not back with a man in 2 months, she's going to hang you." My voice was stricken with guilt.

Wilbur grabbed my shoulders and gave me a gentle but firm shake. "Don't come back, Lilith, I'll be fine, and if I'm not... well..." He trailed off, "...If I'm not, don't worry about that, either. This is your chance, Lilith. Get out of here and never look back."

I stood up from the stool. "I'm not going to let you die, Wilbur!"

"This is your chance to get out while you can. Take the King's horse, Saturn. He's the fastest in all Utuk." Wilbur quickly threw a saddle on Saturn. He was a beautiful black stallion with a cotton white tail.

"I can't leave Carac, either!" I said while Wilbur worked.

"Oh, yes, you can." He said gleefully, smiling.

I shook my head, there was no convincing Wilbur I wasn't going to return, so I ran to the stables to tell Carac of the events that had just taken place.

Carac was weaving a basket.

"Carac!" I yelled out as I ran to him.

I quickly told him what Montgomery had ordered from me as I caught my breath and explained the consequences if I didn't follow them.

"Have you lost your mind?" He said, blankly. "You cannot go throughout the entire kingdom by yourself in 2 months. There are nomads, barbarians, and who knows what else," he insisted.

"I will follow the river, I will be fine," I told him. I kissed his cheek.

19

He looked up at me "I worry about you... You know, no one else here is even worth talking to, Lilith. You are my favorite".

The words he said sent me into a daze for just a moment. Then, he followed it up by saying I was the best choice among the options he had. That comment angered me.

"What is that supposed to mean?" I asked, accusingly.

"Lilith, if the king's horrible guards didn't capture me, I would have my own village right now. My intelligence is wasted here." He said, in a patronizing voice.

I just stared at him. "And you don't think mine is?" I asked.

He didn't say anything, but I didn't think he realized just how awful he sounded.

"I just mean I am above everyone here. You're a good person, Lilith. But, you must understand..." he said slowly.

"Well, I don't," I said blankly. I just stared at him for a moment and then turned and walked away. I couldn't believe I let his words cut me so severely. The worst part was he was still my favorite even with his cutting words...

Detrix came running out of the castle in tears. "Are you leaving, Lilith?" He asked through his tears. I grabbed his shoulder to get his attention. "I'll be back, don't worry, Detrix.

Wilbur came out of the stables with Saturn ready to ride. I turned the reins and looked at Wilbur.

"Take care of him for me, okay," and looked back at Detrix.

Wilbur nodded. I wiped the tears from Detrix's face. "Detrix, until I get back, Wilbur is going to be your best friend so that you won't be alone. Okay?"

Detrix nodded. I gave him one last hug and walked Saturn out of the castle gates.

I climbed on and hit his rump. He started running toward the river. I felt scared. I had rarely left the castle courtyards. The few times I had ventured out into the Kingdom, Felix had always been with me. I wished he was with me this time. But, then again, if he had been, I wouldn't have ended up as Montgomery's slave, and my life might have turned out differently.

Saturn ran for what felt like miles until we were so far away from the castle I couldn't see it anymore. It felt strange to be alone. It felt quiet. I didn't like it. I always had someone to talk to from the time I awoke to the time I went to bed. I had so many thoughts I couldn't share with anyone. It was starting to grow dark, so I decided to stop for the night. I went deep into the forest and tied Saturn to a tree. I sat down and leaned up against a large sassafras tree. I could smell the spicy, earthy aroma emanating from the tree's roots. I slowly laid my head on its roots and drifted off to sleep.

CHAPTER 4: THE KNIGHTS

I awoke dazed and confused to a little tongue licking me on my face. I opened my eyes to a small dog of sorts. This was a tiny little brown dog. It had a little black nose that looked like it had been pushed into its face. I set up, and it sneezed and misted me with wetness.

"Such an ugly little thing," I thought to myself. It started barking at me and wheezed in between.

"Stop it, you little squirt," I said to it.

Then, it ran into the woods. I just looked at the spot it had been for a moment, wondering if I was delirious and it wasn't real. "It must belong to someone," I think to myself, "Nothing that helpless can make it on its own."

Saturn was happily munching grass when I got to my feet. I placed his sattle onto his back and climbed on.

I couldn't get my mind off that little dog. "Where had he gone? He must live near a village." I was trying to reason with myself that the dog was indeed real.

I decided to follow the little dog's trail through the woods, I led Saturn slowly so I wouldn't loose track of it. There were a few tall trees, but the area was dominated by low-growing greenery near the ground. I kept my eyes on the ground so I could see the little paw prints through the mud. I suddenly looked up and there was the little dog again. Just staring and snorting as it breathed. As if it had been waiting for me. She barked at us as if she wanted us to follow her, so we did. "This creature could be leading us to our death," I thought to myself. We were now out of the woods and in a meadow. The grass in the meadow flowed like ocean waves. Across the way, about half a mile away, I could see what looked like a small fortress, with a similar architecture to the castle. When I reached the fortress, I could see women. About twenty. They had what seemed like an armory laid out in the grass and were sharpening all the blades. They had Axes, Bows, Arrows, swords, flails and any other weapon you could imagine.

One woman looked up, "Young Maiden, have you come to join us?"

I was very confused. "Who are you all?" I asked the group.

One woman stood up. She had blonde hair that was braided down her back with leather. A scar over her left eye. We are the "Knights of Utak." She shouted as she put a fist over her chest. "I am Eba!" she said, as if it were a command.

"I thought only the men were the knights," I asked sheepishly.

Ebba nodded in sorrow and then spoke up, "They all died in battle years ago. We are the wives and sisters of the fallen knights. This place used to be a haven until the barbarians came and tortured and killed our men. We all lived here within the knight's fortress. We saw how the men trained and how they fought, and when they fell, we took their place. After word broke out that we were a group of female warriors, others came and joined us searching for an alternative lifestyle, than the traditional life of a woman in the kingdom."

"So, if you haven't come here to join us, why are you here?" Asked Ebba

"What I have come for, I don't believe you can help me with," I let out a small laugh. "I have been sent on a quest by Queen Montgomery, herself, to find her a husband."

All the women looked at each other for a moment and laughed so hard that I almost felt the ground rumble.

One women spoke up, "That Frog thinks a man would want to wed her? There is not a man in the kingdom who would come within ten paces of her. She is the embodiment of evil."

I wondered why the knights felt this way. I knew why I did; she had been truly awful to me, but what had she done to them? I think the knights could see the surprise on my face.

"She has been increasing taxes double or even triple what the king did. King Felix was known for his bloodlust, but he was fair to his own people. If we can't pay, she takes whatever we have as payment, including our grain and meat. If one doesn't offer her something in return for her large tax increase, she has them killed or kills their family in front of them," Added another woman.

My heart pounded as I thought of the danger Wilbur was in. I was shocked. I had been a servant for so long, and since I had never ventured outside of the castle walls, I had no idea what life was like outside of it. The life that the people were living was as bad as that of the slaves. The slaves might even have it better than they did. We at least had food rations.

"This sounds so awful. I am speechless. I need to sit down for a moment to absorb all the information." The news had overwhelmed me.

A woman came over and placed a hand on my shoulder. "I'm sorry, I know this is a lot just to hear. You can do something about this, though. You can join us. We are all planning to invade the castle once all our weapons are finished. We are going to kill Montgomery and take the goods in the castle for the people of Utuk."

I felt it in my bones. My life as I had known it was about to change. I could have trained with those women, taken over the kingdom, and become a hero for the people, but what if the women had been killed as soon as they entered the castle by the guards? I could have left then and continued my search for a husband for Montgomery. I could have run back to the castle, told Montgomery everything, and hoped to gain her favor or I could have joined them but what if they had been liars, only wanting to take over the castle so they could seize control?

"Could I stay a few nights here before I decide?" I asked.

"That's fine, maiden. Feel free to stay with us for the day and observe our lifestyle. You can have a bed to sleep on, and your horse shall have hay and a stable," Ebba offered.

That was an offer I couldn't refuse. I hadn't been in a real bed since Felix had died.

"I appreciate your kindness," I said.

CHAPTER 5: LUCA

Later in the day, I decided to explore the grounds and see the entire fortress. It was smaller than the castle, but like the castle, it has was built to withstand harsh weather.

I walked through the sleeping quarters first. Red poles were arranged throughout the fortress with hammocks strung between them. I ran my fingers along the blankets, and they felt worn and soft to the touch. They were not like the scratchy blankets made from coarse animal hair I was used to. I slowly peeled back the covers and felt the coolness of the linens. I sat down for a moment in the hammock. It was so lovely. I slipped off my sandals and slid in under the covers. I stretched my legs, feeling the softness against my skin. I suddenly felt tired. I wanted to explore the whole fortress, but this hammock was just so comfortable. I felt my eyelids fluttering, trying to stay awake. So, I closed them and felt myself slipping into sleep. I don't think I was asleep long when I awoke to a small tongue licking my hand. I looked down, and it was the little dog again. She just sat down and stared at me like she wanted something. I bent down to pet her when I noticed two large feet standing by her, which startled me.

Just then, a loud voice said, "Umm hello. Who are you, and why are you in my bed?

I immediately jumped up and straightened my clothes. It was then that I looked up at the stranger.

It was a man. He was tall. He had dark olive skin and hair to his shoulders. His hair was curly and waved down his back. He had deep brown eyes that seemed to look into my soul. He looked no more than 20 years of age. He was so attractive, I was at a loss for words. I hadn't seen many men in my time especially my age.

"I am so sorry, sir. It just looked so comfortable." I hung my head.

"Well, normally I don't like strangers sleeping in my bed, but my companion seems to like you, so I will have to forgive you this 1 time." He smiled at me in a resuring way.

"Companion?" I asked him.

He points to the tiny dog creature.

"Oh," I said. "Is that a dog?"

"Oh, Carrot isn't just a dog," he said with an eyebrow raised. "Carrot can take one sniff and know your character."

I was not so believing. "So, you are telling me this creature that sneezes as she runs can tell me if I am a good person or not?

"Well, I am not so sure anymore of her testing methods because I found a strange girl in my bed that still hasn't told me her name." He said with a smile.

"I am Lilith, and I am truly sorry about that…" I said slowly.

"Well, I am Luca, and you are forgiven. But why are you here?" He asked.

I quickly told him about Montgomery's request for me to find her a husband and about the knights, and how I was trying to decide whether to join them.

"You would be an excellent husband for the queen!" I said quickly. "You're very tall and lean, but not too lean, and you look strong. I'm sure you could produce a good seed for the queen!"

Luca laughed, "I wouldn't have that frog as a bride, but I do appreciate your comments about my…seed,"

I felt nervous, and a little embarrassed realizing everything I had just blurted out.

"I thought all the knights were women?" I asked him.

"Well, I am knight, but they just don't like to admit I am of age to be a knight. My Moms don't like the thought of me marching into battle like the others before me." Said Luca

He was younger than most of them...

"Was your father a knight?" I asked him.

"I don't know who my blood father was... I was told when I was a small baby that my mother, who was extremely sick, took me to the knights and begged them to raise me in the ways and arts of the knights. The entire group decided to raise me equally among all of them. So, in a way, I had twelve fathers. But I lost them all. He hung his head. My mothers have taught me well, though." He put a fist towards the sky and made a large circle above his head in remembrance of his fathers.

"Your Mothers seem very brave," I added.

"Oh, they are... Everyone has bravery inside of them somewhere, though." Luca said confidently.

That made me smile.

"Hey Lilith, how about I show you around the villages. I have been instructed to stay out of the way today while they prepare all the weapons. I could handle it myself, but you know, Moms..." He said, rolling his eyes.

"Oh, understandable," I said. I wanted to tell him I didn't know.

I had raised myself, but I felt like this wasn't the best time to say to him I was a slave. I was excited to have a new friend, and I feared that if he truly knew me, he might not want have wanted to be my friend anymore.

"That sounds great," I said quickly.

We walked to the stables. The grass was long and was waving back and forth in the wind on the hills around the fortress like waves.

When we reached the stables, there were so many horses. They all looked beautiful. Luca walked to the back of the stables and walked a large yellow horse with white speckles out into the grass. She was a female horse. She had a sense of calmness about her. Luca got onto his horse and reached out to me for me to hop on. "I have my horse I tell him," I pointed to Saturn.

"Let your horse rest," he said. He will do okay without you for a few hours, and he gave me a wink. I looked back at Saturn, and he was comfortable. He was eating his hay with another horse. She was a mare, too. If I didn't know better, I would think he was happier there then them back at home in the castle's barn.

"Okay," I said and reached out to Luca. He pulled me up like I weighed nothing.

He turned his head back. "Hang on tight. Once she starts going, she won't slow down."

"Okay,' I said. I reach around Luca's waist. I could feel all the muscles in his back and stomach.

I felt myself leaning closer as we rode. It made me nervous to be so close to a man I barely knew, but it also felt so natural, like we rode like this every day. I could smell him. He smelled like a forest of pine and cedar trees. I felt a surge of guilt to be so close to a man that wasn't Carac. Carac was my entire world, but it was also the only world I had ever known.

We rode for quite a while, and then we came to a small village. When they saw us, they began waving excitedly. Luca got off his horse, tied her up, and then helped me down.

An older woman walked up to Luca and handed him a roll wrapped in cloth, "For you, Luca," she paused, lowered her head, and said. "May it give you strength."

"Oh, Mabel." He said, looking down at the rolls. "Please keep your rolls for you and your grandchildren." He said as he put the rolls back in her hand, closed her fingers around them. "I have enough food from the forest." He smiled reassuringly.

Just then, a little boy and girl ran into Luca and grabbed his legs to tried to anchor him down.

"My Goodness, you all are getting big..." He said as he took large steps with both children latched onto his legs. They both giggled.

I looked at all their faces. It was so crowded and noisy. They all seemed so happy. Their happiness was almost contagious. I still couldn't help but notice their gaunt faces and stomachs. None of them had eaten enough for an exceptionally long time.

Once Luca had taken the children off his legs, he turned and looked at me, then at the group of people who had gathered around him. "Everyone, this is Lilith! She is considering joining the knights."

I heard a very loud, like a chant, "Hello Lilith!"

"Hello everyone!" I said a little embarrassed that I was the center of attention.

A middle-aged man approached Luca. I saw him whisper something in Luca's ear, and Luca just shook his head in response.

A While later, the children got caught back into their games, and the adults began slowly going back to their everyday work.

It was then that I asked, "What did that man ask you earlier?"

Luca hung his head. "He asked how the knights were doing and if we had made any progress toward overtaking the Kingdom. The queen's guards took the last of his chickens, and he's frightened they will come back, and he has nothing to give."

"Oh, I see," I said. I remembered the feast of chicken Mongomery and the guards had last week.

"Don't worry about that now, though. I have things to show you," he said as he almost skipped ahead of me.

"Have you seen a blacksmith before?" he asked.

"No, I haven't," I replied.

"Well, today is your day." He took me to the blacksmith across the cobblestone road.

It got warmer the closer we got. He had axes, pots, armor, and necklaces lying in a circle around his shed.

Luca picked up one of the pendants. It was a small depiction of waves. "How much?" He held it up to the Blacksmith.

"A pendant is free when it's for you, my friend," said the blacksmith.

He said and continued to hammer into the pot he was working on.

Luca pulled money out of his satchel and put it into the money pot, then returned the pendant to his satchel.

"It's quite amazing he can make something so blank into something someone will use every day," Luca said.

"It is. I had always wondered how all these things were made." I said as I marveled at the blacksmith's work.

Just then, I looked up and saw a Wagon. It was overflowing with color. It didn't look real to me. It had to be the nomads Felix had warned me to stay away from.

"Luca! Look Nomads! We must tell everyone!" I warned.

"Oh, they are harmless for everything but your wallet," he said, rolling his eyes.

"Won't they steal us blind?" I asked him.

"No, just don't ask for your fortune to be read or for snake oil," he said with a smirk.

"Come with me." He took my hand, and we ran towards the nomads.

BACK TO THE CASTLE: PART 1

Marquise strolled through the stable admiring the horses. He stopped and looked at Saturn's empty stall.

He was a slender man with a thin mustache that gracefully sat on his upper lip. His hair was always tightly pulled back. He moved swiftly, and every move he made was calculated.

"Wilbur, where is the King's stallion?" Marquise asked.

Wilbur shrugged his shoulders. "At this point, I'm not certain. Have you spoken to the queen, sir?"

"Not yet." Replied Marquise.

Wilbur thought for a moment, thinking of how to describe why the horse was missing. "The queen has sent Lilith on a mission to find her a husband."

Marquise hung his head in disappointment. "The queen can be as foolish as Felix."

Wilburn was careful not to show any emotion.

Marquise composed himself. He didn't typically share his personal feelings with the servants. Or now slaves, as Montgomery called them. At times, he did let his true feelings slip around Wilbur. He, after all, had known Wilbur since they were young men.

Marquise was the head guardsman. He was the best guard in all Utuk now that the King was dead. Marquise had always been an advisor of sorts to the king, and now he found himself in the same position as his daughter, Montgomery. Unfortunately, Montgomery was even less receptive to his wisdom than the king was.

While Marquise was busy in the stables, Montgomery looked down at the scattered bits of glass doll strung about the room.

It was then that Carac entered Montgomery's quarters.

"Pick up this glass," Montgomery motioned with her fingers.

Carac nodded and quickly dropped to his knees and began picking up the splinters of glass that had spread across the wooden floor.

Montgomery watched him for a moment before she sat down at her vanity. She continued to watch him, but only from his reflection in the mirror.

"I guess you're mad at me for sending away your little friend Lilith," she said while watching him.

Carac stopped for a moment before speaking, "I am sure whatever you requested of Lilith is of the utmost importance, my queen."

"She might not even be alive right now," Montgomery added and then giggled a bit to herself.

Carac felt sweat drip from his forehead. He didn't know how anyone could stand to be in this draftless room all day and night. He wasn't exactly paying attention to the Queen. He was solely focused on picking up all the glass bits. If she cut her large feet on even a sliver, he would feel her wrath.

"If you are warm, you can unbutton your blouse," Montgomery said.

Carac, for the first time, looked at the queen. "My majesty, I wouldn't want you to have to look at my bare skin."

"Take it off," ordered Montgomery with a not-so-feminine tone.

Carac unbuttoned the blouse. He felt relief from the heat, but he felt enraged that she watching him.

"I said, take your blouse off," Montgomery said plainly.

Carac stood up, took off his shirt, and placed it on the floor next to him.

Montgomery snarled and grabbed a dish of walnuts from her drawer and began to crunch on them.

"You know I can see the orchards from there," as she pointed to the balcony. "When the moon is full of light, I sometimes watch you and Lilith in the orchards."

"Are you going to punish me?" Carac asked.

"No, I just want you to know that I know what you are capable of," Montgomery sneered.

Carac was without words. He put the last of the glass in a waste basket.

Detrix slowly crept into the room. Montgomery hated it when he did that. She didn't like him sneaking around her. She also didn't like looking up and nearly fainted from seeing the near ghost of her late father. Detrix looked increasingly like him by the day.

"What do you want, Detrix?" she asked flatly.

"I wanted to tell you I was sorry I broke your hair." He said and hung his head.

Montgomery let out a huff of air. "Detrix, you <u>CUT</u> my hair, and I know that you know better. That's the second time you've done something like that. You're embarrassing, Detrix, if you can't learn better. I'm locking you up where I won't have to look at you."

"Please don't, I want to be with you, sister, and my friends." He pointed at Carac.

"That is a slave, Detrix! You are supposed to be a prince, but somehow, I got a fool for a brother." Montgomery got up from her seat.

"Go to your room, Detrix. I have had enough of you for one day," she said as she pointed to the door.

Detrix's nostrils flared. "Father said I didn't have to stay in my room."

"Detrix, should I order the guards to dig up the corpse of our father for you to see whatever he said finally doesn't matter anymore?" She screamed at him.

Detrix huffed and barreled towards Montgomery, his arms extended outwards.

Carac leaped forwards, putting himself between the two of

them, stopping the blow.

Carac tried to stop, but it was too late; they both tumbled to the floor.

Montgomery yelled out for the guards to come. They ran into the room and scooped Detrix up off Carac.

"Take him away where my eyes don't have to look at him. Take him to the south tower of the castle." She ordered.

Carac lay on the floor for a moment, regaining his breath.

Detrix pulled at his arms, held behind his back. "That's where the bad people go, and they don't come back." He screamed in horror.

"Good for you, Detrix, you're finally learning something," Montgomery sneered.

The guards took Detrix away. Carac's heart raced, not knowing what was coming next.

Montgomery stood over him and extended her hand out. Carac took it timidly. He could feel her soft palms that had been absent from labor.

"Your good deed will not go unrewarded, Carac." She said in a whisper.

She looked at him and took a finger across his jaw. "I could see why the slave girl likes your company in the orchards," she whispered in his ear.

Carac was holding his breath in fear that the queen was toying with him for a strange amusement. He was desperately holding out for hope that he had truly caught the eye of the queen. He felt sick to his stomach at the thought of reaching out and touching the queen back, but the feeling of being desired was never unwelcome.

CHAPTER 6: THE NOMADS

A s we got closer, I could see their Wagon. The top was painted red, and the wheels were yellow. The horses had purple and green fabric with beaded tassels in place of their saddles. The man driving the wagon was dressed in a red blouse. He had a gold ring in his ears and nose. His curly hair resembled the color of salt and pepper. It was quite a sight. He looked to be in his early forties and beautiful in a way I didn't know a man could be. I had never seen so much color in one place.

"Luca, Luca, Luca, who is this? How many girls have you taken down here this week? Is this the fourth? Or fifth?" The man jumped off the wagon and winked at me.

Luca rolled his eyes. "I won't have you tarnishing my good name to my friend," he said and pointed at the man's face.

The man bent down to one knee and kissed my hand. "I'm sorry you've been in such ravaged company today, but I assure you that you are in good hands now. My name is Piper!" He rose, and as he did, his eyes grew serious for the first time. "You look like a dear friend of mine," he said, grasping my face in his hands. I felt nervous, as if he could peer into my mind and see my thoughts, like words on a page.

Luca, not sensing Piper was serious, playfully pushed his shoulder. "Stop it, Piper! You're gonna scare her away. Don't you start spouting your mystic garbage that you knew from a past life when you were both lizards. We aren't falling for it."

Piper didn't seem to notice, he just kept looking at me and then shook his head like he had been in a trance, and he was trying to clear it from his mind.

"It must just be a combination of a colorful imagination and wishful thinking," he said, and finally let go of my face.

"Nice to meet you, Piper," I said reluctantly. A little frightened at what this overly enthusiastic man was going to do next.

"Where are you two staying the night? The night will soon be with us," asked Piper.

Luca looked at me. "It has gotten quite late." Luca trailed off. "Time seemed to slip away from us today."

"It always does when you're in beautiful company," Piper chuckled and looked in my direction. "Come stay with us. Our humble camp is right outside of town on the other side of those trees," He pointed in the general direction.

"Sure, but no funny business!" Luca said.

Luca grabbed his horse, and we rode behind Piper. It felt natural to be clinging to Luca's waist.

"Luca… How do you know you can trust them? He seems strange. I always heard nomads were dangerous people." I whispered in his ear.

Luca leaned back to whisper in my ear. "Trust me, other than selling overpriced goods or telling fortunes, nomads are good people. They work hard, and they don't have homes like most do. They made their living traveling and selling certain goods to groups of people who might not typically have access to them. I have bought many silks from them for my clothes."

I nodded my head, taking in all the information. There was so much to learn about outside of the castle.

We were getting closer. I could see about twenty tents in a large circle. The tents were all assorted colors.

Even though it had grown dark, the nomads were quite busy. Small children were running everywhere. A group of about fifteen people were beading necklaces. One man was smashing grapes for wine. 3 or 4 older women were weaving fabric. One large man was polishing a transparent sphere.

Piper motioned to his village. "Take a look around. Our home is your home."

We walked through the village and admired all their work, which was beautiful. I couldn't imagine why the royal family had such drab colors in the castle when fabrics like this were available.

Piper clapped his hands three times, and everyone started coming around the fire. Great work. "We made 40 coins today!" The whole village cheered! Luca shouted, "43!" And handed one of the older women three coins, took a small, beaded necklace, and placed it around my neck. I grasped it in my fingers tightly.

They all got up and started dancing and singing. Two or three men grabbed drums and began creating a beat for the party.

Luca grabbed my hand, and we began dancing as if we had become nomads ourselves. One man handed us a wooden chalice of wine. Luca looked at me, shrugged, took a sip, and shivered. I took a sip, but it was too bitter for me, too.

We danced well into the night till our feet were sore.

After everyone had gone to their tents to sleep, Luca and I laid down on a large rug by the fire and looked up at the stars.

"Do they have parties every night?" I asked Luca.

"Yes," he said with a laugh. "They are the happiest people I know. I don't think I could be a nomad myself, but I like to dip my feet in their waters occasionally."

"Beautiful, isn't it?" Luca said. As he looked up into the stars.

"Yes, it is. This has been the best day ever." I said a little too quickly.

"Really? Aren't you some kind of royalty?" asked Luca, "since you were sent from the queen?"

A hot ball of anxiety formed in my stomach. I didn't want to tell him the truth, but he had been so kind, I felt like I had to be honest with him.

"I'm just a slave. I am referred to only as a slave girl at the castle, and if I don't return to the castle with a husband for Montgomery, the horrid frog, she is going to kill my friend, who is also a slave." I held my breath waiting for his response.

"I want to help you, Lilith. I know I just met you, but I can't stand the thought of you taking care of Frog for the rest of your life. You deserve so much more. There shouldn't be slaves in the kingdom at all. The Royal family has enough coin to pay their workers, and we will find a way to save your friend," he said, spitting the words out quickly without much thought.

I could feel anger in Luca, but unlike Carac, I wasn't scared at all. It was almost comforting. He was angry on my behalf and not at me.

Just then, Luca slowly put his hand close to my hand and started weaving his fingers into mine.

I was glad it was dark, and he couldn't see the rediculous smile on my face.

"None of our problems can be solved tonight, so we should go to sleep," I said.

"You are right, my moms told me never to contemplate big problems before bed," Luca said with a chuckle.

"Good night, Luca," I said as I tightened my grip around his hand.

"Good night, Lilith. Thank you for coming with me today." Luca said.

That made us smile even more.

For a moment, Carac's cool blue eyes filled my thoughts. A memory came rushing back of him brushing my hair back when Montgomery had demanded that I eat spoiled food for her entertainment. He had told me I was going to be okay and soothed me to sleep that night with a story from our book, just as I used to listen to the queen when I was a child.

However, the moment was fleeting, and I quickly fell asleep listening to Luca's breathing.

CHAPTER 7: BEAUTY

When we awoke, the sun was shining brightly... Very brightly. The Nomads were back to work with their beads and crafts. I pondered how they could be so chipper after drinking every night.

Luca leaned up, he was squinting, and his hair was going in every direction. He looked down at me and smiled. "Your hair looks funny," he said in a groggy tone.

"So does yours," I giggled.

I leaned up and stretched my arms wide.

Luca stood up, knocked the dirt off himself, and offered me his hand.

I took his hand, and he hoisted me up.

"I guess it's time for us to go," I asked .

"Right after we do some shopping." He winked in my direction.

"Shopping?" I asked.

Luca took my hand and walked in the direction of an older woman with stacks of silk. She was very concentrated on her sewing.

"Which one is your favorite?" He asked.

"Luca, what is this for?" I asked.

"Well, for you, of course!" He cheerfully responded.

"I can't accept such a wonderful gift. I wouldn't even be allowed to wear this at the castle." I whispered.

"Well, good thing you're not going back there," He whispered back and handed me a fabric.

"You know my situation, I must go back for my friends. I don't have a choice." I responded sharply, and I folded the fabric up carefully and put it back.

Luca carefully took my hand. "We will figure out together how to save them without you living a life of misery."

My heart softened, "Even still, I can't have you waste your money on silly clothing for me."

"We aren't leaving until you pick one," he said.

I looked over the fabrics. Each one was different. The next one was more beautiful than the one before. I searched until I saw a deep purple one, which I had only seen in flower petals.

"This one," I pointed out.

Luca smiled and handed it to the older woman. "The full package," he said, and looked at me.

The woman nodded. She took my hand and led me into a tent. I saw Luca giggle as I was whisked away, confused.

The woman began measuring every bit of me with a string. She measured me from my toes to my ears. Then she whistled and, like magic, twenty women came into the tent and began cutting and sewing.

I sat down on a stool while the women worked.

Surprisingly fast, they presented me with a beautiful blouse and matching pants. The pants were tied in the front with slits down both sides. They were beautiful.

I quickly threw my old clothes aside and put on the new garments.

The women all stood back, smiling and nodding to each other, admiring their work. I thanked them and then left the tent.

One woman stopped. "It's missing something."

Another woman grabbed some earrings. "Perfect," shouted the first woman.

I shook my head. "My ears aren't pierced."

"Sit," said the elderly woman as she grabbed a needle from her sewing box.

"Oh, I don't know," I said cautiously.

"Oh nonsense," said the woman.

"Bite down on this," She handed me a leather piece.

I looked at the earrings. They were beautiful, a novelty I had always wanted. As a child, I had played with the queen's earrings in her jewelry cabinet with Montgomery. I had always wanted earrings, but I had never dared to entertain the idea. If Montgomery found out I had done something like that to draw attention to my beauty, it would have been over for me.

I took the earrings in my hands and looked down at them. "Do it!" I said as I handed them back to the woman.

I bit down on the leather as they pierced my ears.

I felt a pinch, but my heart was beating too fast to feel the pain. A young girl brought me a mirror and handed it to me. I looked back at my reflection. Although there were mirrors in the castle, I couldn't get caught staring at my reflection.

I smiled at myself, looking at my ears with the small golden hoops. I felt free.

The women all nodded approvingly at each other at their good work.

I handed the mirror back and walked out into the light.

I found Luca talking to Piper. Luca stopped talking and stared, bewildered.

"Wow," he finally said. "Did you have those before?" He asked, pointing at my ears.

"No," I replied.

Luca turned to the older women who led me inside the tent. "How much for the earrings?" He asked.

"Free earrings for all of Luca's friends," she said a bit mischievously.

Luca's brow furrowed. "She's kidding," He quickly spouted to me. "They have all known me since I was young, and they take every opportunity to tease me," he explained.

Luca tapped Piper's shoulder. "We should be heading back to my mother. They might be getting worried."

Piper's eyes turned serious. "Let me know what they have planned for a castle invasion. I'll help in any way I can. The horrid queen took someone I loved away from me.

"Who?" I asked.

Piper pondered for a moment. "It's a long story I don't have time to tell, but now I loathe the queen, and I don't care if she's young enough to be my daughter. I would slay her in the streets if I could," he said with anger.

Luca's face matched the seriousness of Piper's tone. "The knights are going to spear the frog and everyone who has joined in with her in her evilness."

My stomach sank a bit. I couldn't explain it. My world was changing amazingly fast. A thought of running back to the castle to give warning in hopes of being rewarded with my freedom and the other slaves' freedom crossed my mind, but Montgomery had never been generous. Why would she be now? The thought left my mind as soon as it came.

BACK TO THE CASTLE: PART 2

Montgomery looked out across her courtyard. "Slave boy," she shouted.

Carac jumped to his feet, sprinted to her side, and knelt at her feet. He had found she desired to look at him in this position.

"Yes, my Queen," he said, looking down at the ground.

"Go and pick me a yellow flower in the garden," she pointed towards the yellow flowers.

Carac went out into the garden. He filled his arms with yellow flowers. He put the flowers down at Montgomery's feet. "For you, my Queen," said Carac.

"You may rise," commanded Montgomery.

As Carac stood up, he raised his eyes and looked up at the Queen.

They stood looking at each other for a moment.

"Slave boy, I didn't say you could look into my eyes," She warned.

"I am sorry to be so bold, my Queen, but your beauty was so intoxicating I couldn't help but look at you," Carac's eyes lingered over her body.

A snarling smile ran across Montgomery's face.

"Late tonight, when all eyes have closed for sleep, come to my chambers," She whispered in his ear.

"Yes, my Queen," said Carac as he bowed before her.

Meanwhile, in the south tower of the castle

Detrix set his chin on the cold stone and pushed his face through the bars in the small window. He could only see the leaves on the trees from his window. He felt so lonely. His stomach growled. He walked to the other side of his holding cell. He held two of the bars while he squeezed his face between them.

"When is dinner, James?" He asked the guard.

The guard, James, had red hair. He was thin and pale, but surprisingly skilled in hand-to-hand combat.

James looked at Detrix. "Her majesty said I shouldn't speak to you."

Detrix stuck out his lip. "Please, James, can I have some food? I'll eat whatever you have. You don't have to make me anything special."

James turned around so he didn't have to look at Detrix.

"Jaaamesssss. James. JAMES!" Shouted Detrix.

"Shut up, fool!" James shouted back.

Detrix stopped and walked back over to the small window to look back defeated. He thought about his mom and how she would hold him when he cried. She would tap his back until he was ready to go back to playing. He wished she were here now. He wanted to cry now but was trying to be brave.

James paced back and forth after a few hours had passed. The guards were not accustomed to having prisoners to watch. They weren't sure how to act.

Wilbur appeared in the doorway of the small room holding

two platters with food.

James was startled but relieved to see his dinner.

James pointed at the drumstick on the plates. "Put the meat on my plate and give the bread to the fool."

"The fool is the prince of the kingdom…" Wilbur looked up at James and then cast his eyes down.

"Don't let a sibling spat ruin your career, James," Wilbur warned. 'Montgomery is in control, but Detrix is the Prince of Utuk.

James pressed his lips together like he did when he was pondering something. "Give Detrix one!" He finally spat out.

Wilbur, satisfied, handed James his platter with the drumsticks and stuck Detrix's plate under the bars in the floor.

Detrix reached out and grabbed Wilbur's arm. "Please don't leave me." He begged.

Wilbur touched Detrix's hand softly. "Don't worry, you won't be in there long. Eat your meals for strength." He whispered.

When all had gone to sleep, Carac slowly made his way quietly to Montgomery's royal quarters. He was thankful for the lush carpets to soften his steps.

When he opened the door, Montgomery was lying across her bed. She rolled herself to one side and put her round hand on her chin, resting it there.

"Come up, un-latch my corset," She demanded.

"Yes, my Queen," Carac nearly laughed with glee in his excitement, but in the same breath felt a sickly-sweet feeling in his throat.

Carac began unlatching the clasps. As each one burst open, it gave more weight to the others. By the last button, Carac had to tightly grip the corset with his forearms to release the weight off the final latch.

Once her Corset was completely off, she was left in just her undergarments. They were made from white silk but had faded to a beige color over the years due to use. The garment hugged her sides.

"Carac bring me those berries," said Montgomery, and pointed to a bowl of strawberries on the other side of the room.

Carac brought her the berries.

"Now, fetch the sugar from the kitchen," She commanded.

He ran to the kitchen, not caring if anyone else heard him. He nearly spilled the sack of sugar while carrying it to the queen. He grabbed the bowl she had previously used for the walnuts and dipped out the sugar.

"Now dip the strawberries in the sugar." She demanded.

Carac grasped the strawberry by the stem. He then took the berry to his lips and grazed the tip of his tongue along the tip of the red fruit before taking a small bite, then dipped it in the sugar, and presented it to Montgomery.

Montgomery looked at him, perplexed.

"Those are mine, I didn't say you could have my luxuries, slave boy." She tried to be angry, but a snarling smile ran across her lips.

Carac's heart beat in fear, this crazy plan of his wasn't working. He doubled down, there was no way but through now. He grasped the strawberry again, ever so carefully, licked the sugar off and then rolled it in sugar again, all while he kept eye contact with Montgomery.

He then took the berry and offered it to Montgomery again.

Montgomery raised one eyebrow, then she opened her mouth and closed her eyes.

Carac placed the berry in her mouth.

As she bit down, the juice started to run down her chin, and sugar crushed the corners of her mouth.

Carac took his hand and wiped the drops away from her lips and licked the juice off his fingers.

CHAPTER 8: WEAPONS

I could see the Fortress in the distance on the horizon. As we got closer, I could see the outline of Carrot running towards us with her tiny legs. Luca's horse began turning her gallop into a trot. He gave a slight tap on the reins for the horse to stop. She stopped, and Luca jumped off. As he jumped off, Carrot had reached his feet and was squirming and panting with excitement. Luca picked her up, and Carrot began licking him as fast as she could with her little tongue. "Good girl, Carrot. Did you miss me?" Luca asked in the voice he only used for Carrot.

It seemed unusually quiet. We went inside the fortress to see where everyone had gone. A note had been left on the table. Luca read aloud.

Luca,

We have gone hunting for pelts for the next two days. Help Lilith pick a weapon.

"Well, I guess it's just you and me until they come back," Luca shrugged.

"Let's look at the daggers first," he said excitedly.

The sight made me laugh a little.

He grabbed the weapons and laid them on the large wooden table in the middle of the room. They included two large knives, a bow with arrows, a spear, and a flail.

"Which one catches your eye?" asked Luca.

"My weapon of choice is my longsword. My father forged it himself, even though I don't remember him, I imagine his spirit guiding me through battle," he said in a somber tone.

I picked up the bow and drew it back, feeling the tension, and laid it back down.

I took the knives in both hands, but that felt awkward in my grasp.

I reached over and grabbed the spear, and it felt light in my hands, like it would be hard to control.

So, the axe was left. I grasped it. It felt strong, and I felt stronger holding it. It was the perfect weight, but the flail called me.

I picked the flail and felt its weight in my hands. It scared me, I could easily hurt someone with it. However, the thought also rushed through me that <u>I could hurt someone easily with this weapon</u>. It was a strange feeling of power and fear.

Luca raised his eyebrows. "Flail?" he asked.

I nodded my head.

"Let's go practice," he said excitedly.

He walked out and left inside Carrot, much to her winy protest.

There was a tree that appeared to have been dead for many years, with circles drawn into its wood.

Luca, grasping the flail with one hand, took it behind his head and slowly extended it in front of him. All while carefully looking at the tree.

Luca had been well trained. It landed with perfect accuracy. He pulled the weapon and laid it on the ground.

"Now let me teach you," Luca said with a smile. "It's easier than it looks. We will do it first, just practicing," Luca said with confidence.

Luca came over, pressed his body up against my back, and took my wrist in his hand. "Like this, he moved my hand in a throwing motion."

"Just don't second-guess yourself. That's the most essential part,"Luca said.

We stood for a moment. I could feel Luca's hand wrapped around my wrist gently, and his other hand was wrapped around my waist to keep me steady. I felt the slightest tremble of nervousness come from Luca's fingers.

"Should I try it with the weapon today?" I asked, trying to break the tension.

"Oh, of course!" He said. Luca grabbed the flail's handle and gave it to me. He moved far away from me and the flail's target. "Now try it," he said.

I let it fly into the tree. I wanted to close my eyes, but I kept them wide open.

To my surprise, it had landed right next to Luca's mark in the tree.

My jaw dropped from surprise.

Luca began jumping up and down. "Look! Look what you just did! That is amazing!" Luca exclaimed.

"You are a natural at this," Luca said with a wink. "It took me years to get this good." He said with a tinge of jealousy.

"Let's do this right," said Luca.

He ran back into the fortress with a knight's belt to hold axes on your waist and three more flails.

He fastened the belt around his waist.

"Raise your arms," he said. "I brought a belt for you, too."

He helped me fasten the belt around my waist, and he put three flails on my belt.

"I am thinking, since you are so good at this, we should have a contest." He proposed.

"Alright," I said, "You're on."

We threw the flails until our arms were too tired to continue. It had started to grow dusk.

"My arms are so tired, I don't think I can throw anymore," I said.

Luca wipes the sweat from his brow. "I know just what we need,' he says.

"Come with me. Let's put away the weapons," Luca said.

We put away the flails, and Luca grabbed two blankets from the sleeping quarters.

Luca took my hand as we walked away from the fortress.

'Where are we going?" I asked.

"It's a surprise, don't worry, it's not far," He reassured me.

We walked for another few minutes, only the stars guided our path.

"Okay, here we are. The best-kept secret of the Knights of Utuk. Our hot spring." Luca grinned and extended his arms, showing the hot spring.

I could see a small pool of steamy water.

Luca placed the blankets down close to the pool of water.

"Okay, so now you have to turn around," he said.

I did, and then I heard a loud splash. I turned back around, and Luca was in the pool, and his pants were on the side of the water.

I raised my eyebrows.

"Oh, come on," said Luca. "You can't see anything."

"Well, I can see enough," I said, while laughing.

"Are you going to get in?" Asked Luca.

"Close your eyes," I said.

Luca did.

I slowly slipped out of my new purple silk outfit until all my clothes were lying on the ground.

I then slid my feet into the steamy water. I felt the warm rush go up my spine.

I slipped into the water and let the warm rush take over me.

"You can open your eyes now," My voice seemed to ooze out of me. I was so relaxed.

Luca opened his eyes.

"You look beautiful," he said slowly.

"I thought you couldn't see anything?" I asked jokingly.

Luca looked at me and smiled mischievously.

He put both of his arms on the side of the pool, leaned his head back, and sighed in relief.

The water felt amazing, especially after our long day.

We sat there for what seemed like a long time, just enjoying the water.

Luca looked so strong. I could see his muscles twisting around his arms and shoulders. It was strange to see such a strong person so vulnerable with his guard down.

He caught me staring at him and flexed his arms.

"You ruined it," I giggled.

"Why, I just wanted to give you something to look at if you were going to look," Luca said with a smirk. I was slightly mad at him for the conceited comment, but at the same time, I found him so irresistible.

I had an idea.

"Close your eyes," I told him.

He did.

"Do you have a surprise for me?" He asked.

"Umm...Yes, I'll wait." I replied.

Luca closed his eyes.

Before I had time to think about it, I kissed him on his cheek and then, as quickly as I could, put his clothes on, grabbed mine, and started running.

I had gotten about five paces when I heard Luca yelling.

"Hey! What was that! Where are my clothes!!!" He screamed.

I ran fast until I reached the fortress. I could hear Luca, he wasn't far behind.

I was panting by the time I reached the fortress. When I arrived, I sat down and leaned against the wall, then waited for Luca.

It wasn't long before Luca came through the trees.

He had balled up the blankets into a crumbled ball in front of himself with both hands and was running at the same time.

The sight was so funny that I couldn't help but fall over in laughter.

When Luca finally reached me, he looked like he was trying to make a face like he was angry, but his smile was creeping through.

"Hey! This isn't funny, he said.

"Well, I think it is." I declared.

His face completely changed from a half frown to a giggling child.

"I think it's time for both of us to go to bed," I said.

"I agree," said Luca.

CHAPTER 9: BOOKS

I awoke the next day snug in one of the hammocks. I could see the sunlight creeping through the ceiling. I had no idea how long I slept. I looked down and there was a plate beside my hammock. It was eggs and potatoes scrambled together with rich butter.

I leaned up in my hammock and let my feet dangle below me. I reached down and picked up the plate. Luca must have made this for me. I started eating, and it tasted delicious. The potatoes had the perfect crunchy texture. I heard a small whimper and looked down. There was Carrot.

"Are you hungry, little one?" I asked. She was beginning to grow on me.

So, I picked up a piece of my food and dropped it for her. Carrot quickly gobbled it up and just stared at me then sat down closer to my hammock.

"She's not hungry. She ate half of my breakfast this morning." I heard across the room.

It was Luca.

He came walking in with his wavy black hair that fell into his face. He looked tired, and the day had barely started.

"She's just a little con artist, is all," said Luca as he got up, picked up Carrot, and rubbed her behind his ears.

"How are the stables?" I asked.

"All done," said Luca.

"I was going to help you!" I almost choked on my breakfast.

"I know. I know, but you looked so peaceful." Said Luca and stroked a piece of hair behind my ear.

I frowned. "I could have helped you, though," I said again.

"I have something you could help me with. To be a true knight,

I must memorize and recite the entire Knight's Creed. I was supposed to have already memorized it, but I kept getting distracted," He grabbed a book from the shelf and handed it to me.

"Can you read this and then I will repeat what you said?" asked Luca.

I looked down at the book in my hands. It was a beautiful brown book, bound with strips of leather and crystal white paper. However, I knew I couldn't read, and I didn't know how to tell Luca. So, I thought about it and then said, "Well, I would love to more than anything, but I can't read." I looked at the floor, not wanting to look at Luca, and felt the same shame I had felt with Carac.

-1 Year ago-

Carac came walking into the quarters, rubbing his shoulders.

"Hey, Lilith," he said. "You look excited tonight."

"I am!" Lilith exclaimed. "Wilbur said one of the goats in the courtyard had babies, and one was a little small, so Frog was going to throw it out, but he kept it. We can have our very own goat for milk and everything!"

Carac just shook his head. "Back where I'm from, I have a whole flock of goats. My life is pathetic. I spent my entire day moving the Queen's throne back and forth throughout the castle, only to put it back where it was originally," he said with shame.

"Here, Carac," Lilith said. "Let me rub your shoulders." She had just as tiring a day but felt guilty that Carac could have had a better one.

Carac sat down between her legs on their only stool.

She began pressing her thumbs in a circular motion around his shoulders.

He let out a breath of contentment and smiled.

"I have something for you, Carac," Lilith said.

"What is it?" Carac asked.

"A book. You often say you miss reading the most of all. I hope it's an informative book." She presented it to him with excitement.

"A what? A book?" Carac nearly shouted in excitement.

"Yes," Lilith whispered. "But you must keep quiet. Montgomery had thrown this one away because wine had been spilled on it. If she found out I took it from the garbage, she would be mad."

"So, you brought me garbage?" Carac asked.

Just then, Wilbur rolled over. They both thought he had been asleep.

"Boy, she could have been killed getting that book for you. How about you show a little bit of appreciation?" said Wilbur, then rolled back over.

Carac rolled his eyes in Wilbur's general direction.

"Thank you, Lilith," Carac said. "I do appreciate your effort. It's just that my life will never be what it once was. I'm envious of you because you never knew the difference. You have always belonged to the castle," Carac said with a sigh.

That comment dug at Lilith. Of course, she wanted to be anywhere but here. She changed the subject.

"Please read me something," she said and pushed the book towards him again.

"Fine. That might calm my nerves as well," Carac said.

Carac read her the first chapter of the book. It was so exciting. No one had read to Lilith since the King and Queen.

"Carac, do you think you could teach me to read?" she asked eagerly.

Carac looked down. "I just think it would be too complicated, Lilith. Most people learn to read when they're young by an actual teacher."

"Oh. Okay," Lilith said, hoping not to let on how disappointed she was.

-Back to Present-

"Oh, that's okay." Luca quickly said.

"I'll teach you and then you can help me," he said, smiling.

"Really?" I jumped out of the hammock.

"Am I too old? I thought you could only learn if you were a child." I asked.

"No, not at all," he assured me. "We can start today."

I was so excited I felt like a small child. I had so much joy in my heart, I felt like it was going to explode. Every day with Luca was better than the last.

BACK TO THE CASTLE: PART 3

Carac awoke before Montgomery. The sun was beginning to shine through the stained-glass windows. He put one foot out of the bed onto the lush carpet. He waited a moment to make sure he didn't wake Montgomery. He then slowly slid his body out of the bed. He heard Frog moan, and he stopped. She went back to snoring, so he slowly crept out of her room.

He walked throughout the castles as he ran his fingers along the railings and walls. It was stunning.

He couldn't continue this life of sleeping in the shed with a goat and two other people. He just couldn't.

He had to leave an impression on Montgomery. He had to let her know he was far superior to the others. He had a few ideas, but they wouldn't have a lasting effect, and she would grow bored with him after time passed, even though he had worked to the best of his abilities the night before.

A thought crept into his head. It was perfect, but he really would be sacrificing everything he currently had.

He stopped in his tracks and ran to the slaves' quarters. Wilbur was still asleep. "Thank goodness," he thought to himself.

He crept through the quarters into his area of the room, and there it was. His book. His most prized possession. Lilith had stolen it from the garbage. It was what kept him from losing his sanity. It was the best gift anyone had ever given him. He picked it up and strolled out of the quarters. He felt his stomach turn. He thought he wanted to scream and cry at the same time. He didn't have to do it. He could just put his book back and live out this week in the castle and then go back to his everyday life. He felt so conflicted. He felt a hot tear roll down his face and land on the soft paper of the book.

Thoughts of Lilith ran through his mind. He thought about what it felt like when his fingers intertwined with hers. The way her lips felt brushing up to his ear to whisper a secret. Thoughts of her laugh lighting up even on the cloudiest day. His hands shook. He took a breath and slowly let it escape him.

Carac's mind was made up.

Carac walked straight into Montgomery's room. She was already awake. She was sitting on a stool, rubbing various lotions and oils into her skin. Every single oil had a different floral scent. The smell was so overwhelmingly strong he couldn't smell her odor. Carac didn't know which one would be better to smell.

"My Queen," he dropped to a knee, looking down at the floor. "I have made the most dreadful discovery."

"And what would that be, my Carac?" He asked.

"I went out this morning to start the daily chores, and I found this in Lilith's area. She stole this from you. She was jealous of you. Jealous of your knowledge, your wit, and" He looked up and touched Montgomery's face, "your beauty".

Montgomery gasped. "Oh, thank you, Carac." She took the book and placed it on the table. "Stealing is the first rule of Utuk. She will have to pay to take something unlawfully from the castle. I can't believe she was so stupid," and then Montgomery chuckled. "You know my dear Carac. This is punishable by death, or if I am kind, I will put her in the dungeon, or I am sure the barbarians would buy her for a price."

She stopped talking and looked down at Carac.

"This surprises me," she said as she took her large fingers around his mouth.

"What surprises you, my Queen?" asked Carac.

"That you would betray Lilith. I know that you all worked quite closely together." Her voice trailed off.

Carac took a deep breath and stretched his arms around Frog's neck. He could feel bumps across her shoulders. He looked up into her brown eyes.

"Montgomery, since my time at the castle, the only person I could ever dream of taking a fancy to would be you. Working for you has been such torture. Every night, I dream of walking up to you and touching your skin," he slid one hand down to the small of Montgomery's back.

"OH, Carac," squealed Montgomery. You have proven yourself to me. You shouldn't be in the slaves' quarters any longer. Then she bent down closer to his ear. He could feel her hot breath on his back. "I want you to sleep with me in my bed every night," she whispered.

Carac felt a surge of giddiness. His plan had worked. Lilith was just a slave girl anyway. She had never experienced the best things in life. Protecting Lilith wasn't worth living a life full of darkness.

―

Wilbur was churning butter when he noticed it was quiet, and no one was around. He took a broom from the corner of the kitchen. He began thrusting it into the air, fighting imaginary attackers. He was practicing for his escape. It had been so long since he had held a sword that he wondered if he was still a force to be reckoned with.

Thoughts of his life before becoming a slave raced through his mind. Thoughts of his lover, his friends, and the many faces he had slain. Things he rarely let slip into his thoughts. He knew his life was about to change again. He had been a warrior, a father, a slave, and now he would be a criminal.

———

CHAPTER 10: THE WIZARD

I watched Luca from the doorway of the fortress. He was carrying logs to our oven. Sweat covered his body and soaked through his clothes. Usually, I would have helped, but I couldn't help but watch him do it.

Just then, I felt someone tap my shoulder. I turned around, and it was Ebba.

"Oh, hey Ebba," I said quickly. I was hoping she hadn't noticed me staring at Luca like he was my object.

"What do you think about Luca?" She asked.

Her question completely threw me off. "I think he's amazing!" I said quickly. In hindsight, too quickly. It was hard not to yell from the rooftops about Luca.

Ebba laughed. This put me at ease, and I smiled and laughed with her.

"Does he know?" She asked.

"I don't know…" I said as I trailed off.

Luca looked up from his work, smiled, and then waved at us.

We both waved back.

"You know, he needs someone like you," she said.

"I need him too," I replied.

"I don't think you do," Ebba smiled and almost laughed at me.

I raised my eyebrows at her.

"I think you <u>want</u> him, but I think he <u>needs</u> you," she said.

"Before you came, the only thing he enjoyed was playing with Carrot. Since you arrived, he has risen early every day. He works hard. He smiles more. You give him a reason to live. He was just existing before." Said Ebba, "I know it's only been a couple of weeks, but I feel like we have known you forever."

I couldn't help but smile.

"You should tell him if you love him. And just so you know,…" she paused. "I told him the same thing,".

I didn't know what to say. The comment threw me off. I didn't realize Luca and I had been so obviously enthralled in each other.

"Now, quit staring at my son and help me sharpen these darts," she said with a laugh.

A slight smile escaped my lips, and I grabbed a handful of darts from her basket.

We sat down and began scraping them across sharp rocks, making the points jagged.

As I finished the last dart, Nyx came running inside the fortress and grabbed her sword.

"What's going on?" asked Ebba.

"I spotted the Wizard in the forest close to the villages," She said through gasps of air.

Ebba jumped up from the floor, grabbed her flail off the wall, and ran to the stables with Nyx close behind.

I didn't have time to think, I grabbed my flail and ran to Luca. I quickly told him what I had witnessed, and he grabbed my hand, and we ran to the stables.

We got on our horses. Nyx and Ebba had already gone ahead of us.

We rode our horses fast through the thick of the forest until we came to a make-shift camp. A man stood dressed in a faded black cloak and a pointy black hat. The smell was putrid, like that of dead animals. Rotting flesh just baking in the sun. Dead animal organs and pieces lay around his tent.

Ebba looked down at him from her horse. "Today is your last day, Wizard."

I drew my flail, and Luca motioned for me to stop. "They have this one," he said and pointed to his mothers.

Ebba took the flail from her hip and threw it in the direction of the man with the sword. The spikes tore into his side. The man screamed out in pain, then turned and faced her.

In one fast motion, she jumped off her horse. He breathed in, and I could see his nostrils flaring and the red blood dripping from his side. He charged toward Ebba with his sword extended forward. She threw her flail into the air. I watched as it came crashing down, and the chains wrapped around the man's neck twice. He quickly dropped his sword. I heard the man's neck snap under the pressure of the chains. His last breath escaped his lungs, and he fell to the ground dead. Ebba pulled her weapon from the man's body and placed it back on her hip. Blood dripped from its spikes. She took her foot and moved the man's body to where it was faced up. Ebba looked down at him for a moment, then spat on his face and walked away.

I was speechless, to say the least. I looked at Luca and whispered, "Who was that?"

Luca looked down at the ground. "We have been looking for him for years now. He stole Ebba's baby long ago."

"Did she ever find it?" I asked.

"No," said Luca.

"Oh," I said quietly.

Nyx walked behind Ebba, wrapped her arms around Ebba's waist and placed her chin on Ebba's shoulders.

"They are all gone," whispered Nyx.

Ebba took both her hands and placed them on Nyx's arms and sighed.

Ebba looked at Luca and motioned for him to come close. Nyx let go of her shoulders and walked over to me.

Nyx, unlike Ebba, had noticeably short red hair that was cut like a man's.

Ebba grabbed Luca and grasped him tightly in her arms. Luca grabbed her back and placed his head on her shoulders. She looked small compared to him.

I leaned over to Nyx. "I feel like I missed something major," I said.

"That man took Ebba's child for a sacrifice to his gods for magic. However, he is the last of his kind, and the wizards of Utuk are dead," said Nyx.

"That's awful," I said slowly.

"The child would have been almost 22, now," said Nyx.

"Was it a boy or a girl?" I asked.

Nyx smiled, "A girl."

Luca took his sword from his side and sliced the man's head off his body.

"What are you doing?" I asked.

"I'm going to display this where the villagers can see, with a sign that simply reads 'Last Wizard of Utuk.'"

Ebba got on her horse. Her long braids had come undone from the top of her head and seemed to fall down her back like a waterfall. "Come with me, Lilith," She requested.

I quickly hoisted myself back onto Saturn and came to her side.

We rode back to the fortress in silence for a while. Then she spoke up. "I can't live without knowing Luca is going to be safe," she said.

"I think that's very understandable," I said quietly.

"I know he would go above and beyond to keep others safe, but I need to know you will help keep him safe." She said,

I reached out and grabbed her horse's reins, looking her in the eyes. "I will keep him safe or die trying."

She grabbed my hand. "I believe you."

CHAPTER 11: THE CREEK

L uca went to the creek to wash the blood from his hands. I watched as he sat down in the middle of the large rocks. He stared out into the distance and let his fingers touch the water. I grabbed a bar of soap from the bathing area and slowly walked out to him. He didn't seem to notice I was there, and I didn't want to startle him. So, I slowly reached out and touched his shoulder. He turned and looked at me. I could feel the sadness in his eyes. I bent down in front of him and let the cool water seep into the bottom of my pant legs. I began unbuttoning his shirt for him. His chest was now exposed, so

I slipped it off his shoulders. He brought his hands out of the water and ran his fingers through my hair. My dry hair clung around his wet arms. I dipped the bar of soap into the water and began washing the blood from his chest and began making my way down to his legs. He just watched me. I could feel his deep brown eyes peering into my soul. For the first time, he spoke up. "I can do that," he said quietly.

I looked up at him. "Let me."

I took his shirt through the water and watched as the dried blood created tiny streams in the water and washed away.

"How could anyone take a baby?" He asked quietly.

I shook my head.

I cupped my hands together and poured it over his head. He closed his eyes and took a sharp inhale.

"Do you know what happened to your parents?" He asked.

"No, all I know is that I was born to serve in the castle," I replied.

"Are you curious where you came from?" He asked.

I pondered the question for a moment. "I don't anymore," I said, "I used to, but there isn't any use in knowing who gave me up. I was bought as a present for Montgomery. My parents may have loved each other and been forced to give me up to feed their other children. Or my mother was young and didn't even know who my father was. Either way, that would be a wound I wouldn't want to reopen."

He cupped his hands and poured water over my shoulders. A shiver rolls down my spine.

He moved off the rock and sat down in the water. The waves began rushing over the tops of his legs like his body was now part of the creek.

I sat down in front of him and felt the water pushing against me. He wrapped his hands around mine "Sit with me for a while?" He asked.

I nodded, "Yes".

The cool water felt exhilarating on my lower back on the sweltering summer afternoon.

He closed his eyes, and we let the water rush against our bodies.

We sat in the water till the sky grew dark and our skin wrinkled.

"Luca," I said quietly.

"Yes," He replied.

"Are you ready to go inside?" I asked.

He nodded and stood up. His pants clung to his thighs while the water fell from him.

He pulled me up by my hands.

"You know, I bet Carrot has missed you today," I said quickly.

Luca smiled.

We began walking back home.

Carrot came running to Luca and began jumping up and down, wanting to be held. Luca picked her up and held her close while Carrot squirmed and licked his cheeks.

Carrot stopped for a moment and then looked at me and began barking and grunting at me excitedly. I looked at Luca, puzzled.

"What does she want?" I asked.

Luca laughed, "She wants you to pet her, too."

I smiled and rubbed her ears. Carrot looked up at us, like she was smiling.

Luca placed her on the ground and looked at me.

"I have never felt more at home," I said.

Luca grinned "Neither have I".

"But you have been here your entire life," I said.

"Yes, but you have never been here before," he said quietly, and kissed me on my forehead.

We slowly creeped into the sleeping quarters and changed into dry clothes.

I climbed into my hammock below Luca's and wrapped myself in a blanket.

Luca walked to my hammock and looked down at me.

He bent down to his knees, to where his mouth was close to my ear.

"Can I get in your hammock with you?" He whispered.

A smile escaped my lips "Won't your mothers catch you in here?" I whispered back.

"I don't think they will mind that much…" He trailed off. "Anyway, I will get it into my hammock before they wake up."

I rolled my eyes and patted the space next to me.

Luca slid his warm body next to mine. I felt safe next to him. He reached down and brought my blanket over us both. He placed one arm under my head, and his other wrapped around my body.

"I like the way your hair smells," he said.

I reach and intertwine my fingers with his. "I like you," I said.

He squeezed me tight. "I like you too."

I feel myself drifting into a daze between sleep and awake.

I awoke next to Carac with his arms wrapped around me, with his clothes off again.

I felt a sticky warmth in the air, so I got up from his side and walked around the room. Everything was where I had left it. The air was still, so I decided to wake Carac. I tried shaking his shoulders, but he just lay there, not moving.

"Carac," I tried yelling, but nothing came out of my mouth. I ran to the quarters to find Wilbur to help me wake up, but Wilbur was nowhere to be seen.

I yelled his name, but once again, nothing came out. In pure desperation, I ran to the guards' quarters. Marquise, in his filthy ways, might help me, but I would owe him if I did. I ran anyway, I needed to help wake Carac.

When I reached their lair, I pulled open the doors, and the guards were all there. They were all placed around the table like toy men ready to be picked up and put away. I walked over to one of the men and pushed them. His body felt like a rock, cold to the touch.

I walked over to Marquise and looked at him. He was like stone as well. I reached out and touched where his pinky fingers used to be. When I touched him, a drop of blood fell from his pinky and onto the floor. I looked up at Marquise's still face. His face looked like it was made from wax, unmoving. A smile slowly drifted across his face without his eyes moving.

"You did this to all of us," he said.

I awoke to Luca shaking me awake. "Lilith, you were having a nightmare. Are you okay?"

"I am now," I said as I wrapped my arms and legs around him. "Just hold me."

BACK TO THE CASTLE: PART 4

Carac carefully grasped his fingers around the worn blanket in the slaves' quarters. He brought it close to his cheek to feel the softness. He took a deep inhale, but he couldn't spell Lilith in it any longer. He felt a tightness in his chest that he couldn't control. He grasped the rags of the blanket and tore it apart. The sounds of the threads tearing gave him a rush of sadness and satisfaction. He threw the rags down and began walking back to the castle, back to Montgomery.

When he reached the castle, Marquise greeted him. Marquise looked at him from his feet up to his eyes, like he had been wondering where he was.

"Where have you been?" Asked Marquise.

"I was working," replied Carac in an aggravated tone, and went to walk around Marquise.

Marquise chuckled and then, in a swift motion, grabbed Carac's collar.

"Why are you still looking for hints about her?" Marquise said calmly.

"I wasn't doing anything," Carac wheezed.

Marquise tightened his grip.

"I miss her," Carac spat out.

Marquise released Carac and shoved him to the ground.

Carac fell to his knees.

Marquise paced back and forth in front of Carac.

"I will not have another person treat Montgomery 2nd to that little wretch of a slave." He said firmly.

Carac nodded. "I see the error of my ways, good sir, from now on my loyalty lies strictly to the queen."

"Then we will learn to become friends one day," Marquise offered his hand to help Carac up.

---

2 years prior

Felix bent to pick up a four-leaf clover out of the castle yard. He looked at it in wonder. He acted as if he had never seen one before, even though this was his daily ritual. On the other hand, he was holding his pipe, which took his pain away.

He took a sharp breath of spring air and began walking back into the castle.

Marquise looked down at him from the balcony. He saw how each strand of the King's hair went down his back looked like an ever-curling river. By their age, most of the men had begun to break down, but Felix had just traded his dark hair strands for grey. He now had a beard, but Marquise liked it on him. It fits his personality.

He had to leave soon before Felix saw him here.

Marquise went running down the hall, his long cloak draped behind him.

He saw Felix, so he quickly hid behind a pillar. He watched Felix hand Lilith a clover. They were both smiling.

Marquise looked up and made eye contact with Montgomery. She was standing across the hall. She quietly motioned him closer with her finger.

Marquise looked down at Felix to ensure he was occupied and then ran to Montgomery.

Montgomery walked to her room. Once Marquise was inside, she shut the door calmly.

"Marquise, I need a favor," she said.

"Anything for you, flower?" He said quickly.

"The time has come for new blood in the Kingdom of Utuk." She said flatly with no emotion.

"Your time will come," said Marquise with a smile.

Montgomery stopped and looked out her window. "My father is going to outlive us all. You see how he grows stronger every day, and he is twice my age and shows no sign of it." She closed the curtain, and the room grew grey.

"That's why you're going to kill him for me," she said quietly.

Marquise's blood ran cold.

"I can't kill the King," he said quickly.

"I'll give you your guardsmen ship back. You won't have to beg in the streets any longer like a pervert," she said.

Marquise shifted his weight between his legs and looked down at his missing fingers.

"How? If anyone saw, I would be hanged from the gallows," he said.

"I will tell Felix the Nomads are being attacked, they are his favorites after all…Before he even gets to the village, you will kill him," She stated.

"He will have his guards with him," said Marquise.

"I will tell Felix I have already sent them, and he will be right behind them," said Montgomery as she paced around the room.

The next day, Marquise sat with his knife in his hand where Montgomery had told him to stay. His fingers were trembling. He threw up into the grass next to him. He saw Felix upon a stallion running through the field. Marquise had to take him by surprise. He began running fast towards the stallion. Felix had not even noticed him. Right as the horse was about to run past him, he grabbed Felix's arm and pulled him off the horse. He quickly pinned him to the ground. Felix looked up at him, confused. Marquise brought the knife to his throat. His hand was shaking.

"You can't do that," said Felix with a smile.

"Why can't I?" Screamed Marquise in anguish.

"Because I know you," said Felix, but his words were cut short.

A dart came through the air and landed in Felix's chest.

Marquise turned around, and there was James smiling, holding a large blow dart gun. Montgomery knew Marquise wouldn't finish the job on his own, so she sent James.

Marquise grabbed Felix's hand and looked into his eyes. "Montgomery is my daughter. I am so sorry for everything, my dear friend," Whispered Marquise.

Felix looked him in the eyes and, through a gargled voice, said, "I have always known, and I know you would do anything for your daughter."

He took his last breath and laid his head down.

Marquise gently closed Felix's eyes as tears slipped from his own.

———

"You should know, Carac, that if Montgomery grows tired of you, she won't think twice about ending you… Also, she will always have the guardsmen on her side," Marquise warned.

Carac stood tall. "I'll be her favorite before too long if I'm not already."

Marquise put on his gloves to conceal his fingers. "For your sake, I hope you're right."

That evening, Wilbur slowly crept past James, asleep. Wilbur had filled his dinner with Valerian root and chamomile dressings. He had also brought ale and said it was from Montgomery for good measure.

Wilbur brought his finger to his lips and motioned for Detrix to stay quiet.

Wilbur ever so carefully pulled the Keys from James' belt and unlocked the gate.

Detrix and Wilbur crept out into the night.

Once they had made it back to the barn, Wilbur helped Detrix into the rafters of the barn until he could think of an escape plan. It wasn't ideal, but it would take a while for the guards to check there.

CHAPTER 12: THE CEREMONY

We worked on my reading all afternoon.

"Well, that was good for today," said Luca as he shut the book.

I felt like I was walking on the clouds. I was so excited. I was reading simple sentences, and I couldn't have been happier.

Just then, we heard the roar of horses riding past the door.

We looked out, and it was the Knights.

They had animal pelts and meat dragging behind the horses on a makeshift wagon. Blood from the hunt covered their faces and bodies. They were all laughing as if one of them had just told the most hilarious story as they approached us.

Ebba looked down at us while she twisted her braids onto the top of her head from her horse. "We are going to bathe in the river. Could you two start putting the pelts out in the sun to dry out and put a hog on the fire to roast?" Ebba asked.

Luca and I nodded.

We dragged the pelts into the sun.

As we were beginning to put the meat into the smoke house, Luca turned to me and said, "Since we had such a large hunt, we will have a celebration of the animals and the nourishment that they provided us tonight after sundown," He said with excitement.

"Like the Nomads?" I asked.

"Not exactly, it's more of a ceremony than a party," He explained.

"Well, I am used to that. Living at the castle, I see lots of those." I added.

"I have never been to an official Utuk castle ceremony, however, I don't think it's like that either," he said.

Later that night, just as it began to get dark, all the women started coming out of the fortress. They were all dressed in white cotton tunics, and Nyx was in a red tunic.

They handed Luca and I similar white outfits and told us to change into them.

We went into the fortress to change, and I grabbed Luca's arm once we were out of sight.

"What is going on?" I asked.

Luca grinned, "I can't tell you, but it's going to be a lot of fun."

As I slipped the last piece of material around my chest, I couldn't help but let my eyes linger on Luca. It was as if I had never seen a man before when I looked at him.

The muscles in his legs and back were incredible. I wanted to touch him so badly.

I was suddenly overtaken by fantasy.

Luca came over to me, hoisted my hips onto his. I began running my fingers through his wavy hair. It suddenly felt like all my senses were heightened. He began kissing me and carried me to the sleeping chambers in the castle. He sat down on one of the beds. I could feel his hands running all over my bare back. His hands felt warm like fire, but in the best way. He started kissing my neck, and

I felt weak as if I were melting like butter on a scorching day. He grabbed me tightly, lowered me down onto the bed, and continued kissing my neck and making his way down my chest. He took my hands and grasped them tightly in his, then placed them above my head...

My fantasy was cut short.

"Are you watching me?" asked Luca.

I could feel my cheeks turning red.

Luca laughed "Why are you watching me?" He asked, but he already knew the answer.

"It's as if every man I've ever seen before you was just a shadow," I said quietly.

Luca walked over to me, brushed the hair out of my face, and stared at my lips.

Just then, Ebba opened the door.

"Are you all ready? We are all waiting," she said impatiently.

Luca and I ran out the door.

We were all handed small strips of red cotton material, and then Nyx banged loudly on a drum, silence fell over the group.

In a chanting tone, she spoke, "Tonight you are with the earth and the earth with you."

"Tie the cloth over your eyes." She commanded.

We all did. It was completely black.

Nyx spoke again. "When you hear the drum again, start walking towards the sound. If you listen to the earth, you will be rewarded."

We all stood there. I could feel the cool grass on the bottoms of my feet, and I felt the breeze like it was speaking just to me.

I heard a faint "bong" in the distance. Everyone began strolling towards it. We were all together and alone at the same time.

Every few moments, I could hear the "Bong," and it was getting louder.

I felt the ground change. We were in the woods. I could feel leaves and twigs, so I slowed my pace. I felt the rough bark of trees brushing against my skin and the leaves of trees stretching out and guiding my path, like they could hear the drum too.

Then I heard a "Bong" that was so incredibly close it hurt my ears, and then I felt Luca grab my arm. He bent down close and took my blindfold off. I felt a little off balance.

"Wow, you were amazing. On my first drum walk, I got lost for an hour. My mothers thought I was lost." Whispered Luca

Nyx smiled at me, as if she felt complete peace, and nodded, pleased with my outcome.

I looked across the woods, and I could see there were still a few of the Knights who were going through the forest. I suspected they knew these woods very well, but they were enjoying the journey.

Luca and I continued to tap everyone on the shoulder when they approached the drum until everyone was sitting in a circle.

The Nyx tapped the drum one more time. "Now it is time to celebrate our hunt. She grabbed a bottle of wine that was sitting beside the drum. Drink, my sisters!" She commanded.

Luca smirked as his mother said, "I'm here too." He said, which broke the silence, and everyone laughed.

She corrected herself, "My sisters let us drink and Luca," and raised the bottle.

We took turns passing the wine until I felt like my head was swimming.

"Let us eat!" Said one woman.

We began walking back, and I could smell the pork roasting that Luca and I had started making earlier in the day.

We all took knives and sliced the pork, then ate it until our bellies were full.

"Now let us sleep and dream of slaying our enemies and all the knights!" Nyx shouted in triumph.

I thought about their enemies and hoped none of their enemies were my friends.

CHAPTER 13: LUCA'S SQUIRREL

I awoke before everyone else the next day, and for the slightest moment, I didn't know where I was. I sat up in the hammock and looked over, seeing Luca asleep in the hammock above me made me feel at ease. He looked so peaceful. He had Carrot tucked into the hammock under his arm. I couldn't help but smile. Carrot's eyes were open and watching me but happily tucked away in the hammock.

I slowly crept out of the sleeping chambers. I walked to the stables. It was a beautiful morning. The sun had just kissed the horizon, and a fog covered the grass. The animals were beginning to wake up. I walked into the stables. There was Saturn. He was quietly grazing on some hay. He looked cozy in the stables here. I took him out of his stall and into the grass. He looked at me and then nuzzled my hand to scratch his head. This made me sad because that is what he would do to Wilbur every day. I took a deep breath in and let it out. I thought about Wilbur, Carac, and Detrix, what they were going through while I was gone. I thought about what Carac would think about Luca. I would have a tough time telling him. Carac and I had been together, but at the same time, we were never together. I thought I loved Carac, but after knowing Luca I realized I never had loved Carac. I stopped petting Saturn for a moment.

"<u>I love Luca.</u> How could I let my heart get so caught up in him? Did he love me?" I said aloud to myself.

Carac had made it more than clear that if he weren't a servant, he wouldn't be with someone of the likes of me. "So would he even be upset when I freed him and found out I had found another?" I thought only to myself.

"What am I going to do, Saturn?" I asked him as if he was going to respond.

He just grumbled. I knew what he wanted, so I pulled myself onto his back and grabbed his mane. Saturn was off, trotting down the hillside.

I rode him up and down the hillside until his pace slowed and he was tired, so I guided him to the river where he could drink.

When we reached the river, I jumped off. I was quite parched myself.

I bent down and took handfuls of the water, bringing it to my lips. The water was a perfect temperature for drinking; it felt crisp.

I walked Saturn back to the stables and gave him some fresh hay.

The fog was beginning to disappear from the air. Everyone would be up soon. I decided I would do some of the chores before they awoke.

I gathered the eggs from the chickens and milked the cow.

I thought about the milk goats back home and wondered how they were doing and how the chickens were laying.

After I finished placing everything into the cellar, I saw Luca emerge from the fortress. He was rubbing his eyes.

'Hey Sleepyhead," I said.

Luca was still squinting. "What are you doing?" he asked.

"I just got done milking the cows and gathering the eggs from the chickens," I cheerfully responded.

Luca pushed his lips together. "You know, I was supposed to do all that. I can't have our guests doing all our work."

"Maybe I don't want to be your guest anymore," I said.

"You want to leave?" Asked Luca

"No, I want to stay," I said.

Life seemed to pour into Luca's eyes, and he smiled.

"Everyone is going to be up soon, let's make them breakfast. You know that's what I'm good at. I have been cooking every day at the castle since I was a little girl," I said.

That last part made Luca sad, but he snapped back to himself. "That sounds great. Let's do it!"

"Let's go then!" I said in excitement.

We gathered enough eggs for everyone. Then, while I gathered twigs for a fire in the oven, Luca cracked eggs. I gathered some dandelion greens and chickweed to throw into the eggs as well.

Luca poured the eggs into the pan, and I could hear a sizzle. Then I quickly threw pieces of butter throughout the eggs.

"What's that for?" asked Luca.

"It makes the eggs fluffy," I replied.

Luca looked surprised.

"Okay, keep stirring the eggs, don't stop," I warned Luca.

I went into the cellar and retrieved some cheese, then began slicing it into thin pieces.

I took a piece for myself and ate it.

I took the pieces of cheese and laid them gently on the eggs, letting them melt.

Luca takes a deep breath in through his nose. "That smells amazing," he said.

We took the pan off the stove and began putting bowls on the table.

Just then, the knights began making their way into the kitchen.

"This looks wonderful," I heard one of them say.

They all sat down and began to eat.

I looked over at Luca from across the table, and he smiled at me.

Ebba looked at me. "This is delicious, Lilith," she said, pointing with her fork.

"Luca cooked too," I added.

And they all laughed.

"I know Luca didn't do this on his own," another woman said.

"Sometimes Carrot won't even eat Luca's cooking," someone said.

Luca looked embarrassed. "Please stop."

One of the women looked at him and rolled her eyes.

"Lilith, you want to know something about Luca's first pet?" she asked.

I saw Luca's eyes widen. "No, stop talking," he shouted.

"When Luca was just a youngster, we took him on his first hunt. And we killed a squirrel, and he wanted to keep it," She giggled.

I almost spit out my food while I was chewing, "Like a dead squirrel?" I asked.

"Yes!" Shouted another woman.

"He carried the squirrel around until it was stiff and stank." Added Nyx, crinkling her nose.

"It was then that I finally told Luca he couldn't keep his <u>pet</u> squirrel," Ebba said through laughter.

Luca was bright red. "I can't believe you all told her that! To my defense, you all should have let me get a pet sooner!" He said.

They all looked at him and rolled their eyes.

"Let us finish our breakfast before it gets cold," I said.

Which everyone did. It was a great morning.

BACK TO THE CASTLE: PART 5

Carac yawned as he pulled the blankets back off his naked body. Montgomery was still snoring next to him. He sat on the edge of the bed and looked down at his stomach. It was beginning to take on an outward curve. His body had not looked like this since he was a small child.

He heard a knock at the door.

He quickly threw a sheet around himself and opened it. There stood James.

"I must speak to Montgomery," said James.

"She is still asleep," replied Carac.

'I must speak to her at once. Detrix has escaped," James said this time with hostility.

Carac turned around to tell Montgomery, but she was already out of bed, marching toward the door.

She shoved Carac out of the way and grabbed the guard by the collar of his shirt, pulling him close to her face.

"Listen to me, you fool. You will have my brother back by nightfall if you don't want to be thrown in the dungeon." Montgomery practically spat out.

She then shoved him back through the door and then slammed it into his face.

"My Queen, why not let your brother wander the kingdom? What does he matter?" Asked Carac.

"My brother is still of royal blood, and if a neighboring royalty finds out I have cast out Felix's firstborn son into the streets, our Kingdom will be seized by another one. All our neighboring nations will revolt against us." She cried out.

"I have sacrificed too much for that fool to ruin everything. If he is in the castle, I can pull him out when royalty visits at my convenience, or if I kill him, I will at least know he is not causing trouble. However, killing him would be a last resort."

She sighed.

This was the first Carac had had of this. He had no idea royalty was held to any standards by others.

Montgomery just stood there shaking her head. "He could do other things as well. He could marry and turn a street girl into a princess, He could start a war, he could sell our land, He could do anything I can do. He must console ME before making executive decisions in the kingdom."

"I'm sure they will find him my queen," Carac said in his most soothing voice as he laid back down on the bed, hoping he could ease the Queen's troubles for a moment.

Wilbur was plucking chickens when the guards arrived.

"Have you seen Detrix? He has escaped the Dungeon," shouted one of the guards.

Detrix bowed his head to the Royal guards. "No, I have not, Sir."

One guard looked at him suspiciously. "Are you sure? If we find that you are protecting Detrix in any way, you will be thrown into the dungeon to rot or hanged at the queen's discretion."

The guards looked at each other, then back at Wilbur. They could always spot a liar. They were not imbeciles.

The biggest guard took Wilbur's chin in his hand and brought it to his face. "You're either going to take me to him or you're going to the dungeon now," shouted the guards.

Wilbur spat into the guard's face. He knew his jig was up, but he wasn't going to make it easy.

He took a swift kick to the side of the larger guard's knee. The guard fell to the ground in pain and rage. Wilbur jumped onto the guard's back with one foot on his head and one on his back and crushed him into the dirt. As he jumped, he grabbed the flail off the man's belt and flung it into the other guards' face. He could hear flesh tearing with the metal, and the man screamed out in pain and ran away. A third man came behind Wilbur and grabbed his neck. Two men were down, all he had to do was fight the third. He grasped the Flail with all his might, threw it behind him, and hit the man in the back. The flair was now covered in blood. He heard the man screaming louder and louder. The guard kept his tight grasp on Wilbur's neck. Just when Wilbur felt the light of day beginning to slip away from him, he felt the man let go of his neck. He turned around, and he had gotten a lucky shot to the man's head.

He stood there for a moment, breathing in and out, and then ran to Detrix, but not before he placed the flair on his own belt.

"Come on, no, Detrix!" Shouted Wilbur into the barn.

Wilbur threw saddles on the castle's two best horses and tossed himself onto one while he motioned for Detrix to do the same.

Detrix quickly jumped onto the horse, and they began riding as fast as they could away from the castle.

"Where are we going?" shouted Detrix over the horse's hooves.

Wilbur is still looking off into the distance. "I don't know what lies ahead, but anything will be better than the dungeons of Utuk."

CHAPTER 14: ELIZA

L uca and I laid on the grassy hillside just out of sight of the fortress. I was reading a book to Luca that he had given me to practice my reading. My pace was slow, but each day I was growing in my abilities.

When I finished, I laid the book down and snuggled my head into Luca's arm and looked up into the sky. It was a beautiful day, it wasn't too hot or too cold, and the sun was barely behind the clouds.

"I can't imagine life without you, Lilith," Luca said quietly as he took his arm and pulled me close.

I rolled over and put my arm on his chest. "Don't be silly," I said.

Just then, Luca leaned up to where he was holding himself up with one arm. I could tell he was trying to be as serious as possible. "Really, Lilith, when I wake up, you're my first thought, and when I go to bed, you're my last thought. You never leave my mind. I am completely enamored with you, Darling."

"Darling?" I asked him with a smile on my face, almost laughing. "How many girls have you told that to?" I asked.

Do you want to know? He replied.

"Yeah," I said, and I sat up and crossed my legs.

Luca sighed.

---

1 year ago

"My darling, what are you doing?" Luca said as he laughed.

Eliza stood there swaying back and forth like she was dancing. Her skin glowed in the moonlight as she took a swig from the bottle of wine she had stolen from her father.

It was quite a sight. Her blonde hair swung around her ears, only to make her bright blue eyes more visible. She was wearing only a white sleeping garment that was cut off above the knee and was tied around her neck. She had the type of smile that you couldn't tell if she found you amusing or if she was plotting against you.

"What about it, Luc? Let's run away tonight and never look back, just like we are always talking about. We could go down to the docks and get on a ship and see the world." She moved her hand across the sky like she was looking out at the sea.

Luca rolled his eyes and took the bottle from her hand, and had a long drink. "You know I hate it when you call me that. Luc doesn't sound like a name."

"You're avoiding the subject, Luc. Now come dance with me," said Eliza as she motioned for him to stand up.

Luca stood up and put his hands around her waist. He could feel her hips beneath her skin. She placed her hands around his shoulders and leaned into him, and they began to sway back and forth.

The more they danced, the closer they intertwined till they were pressed so close against each other that they could feel each other's hearts beating.

"Luca... I love you, but when I look into your eyes, I know you don't love me." She said quietly.

"You're drunk, darling, we can talk about this tomorrow?" asked Luca.

"If you loved me, you would say it right now," replied Eliza.

They continued to sway with the wind.

After a few moments had passed, Luca said, "I love you, but I love Utuk and my mothers more. I could never leave this place. I am a Knight of Utuk. This is what I was meant to do."

"What if you die in battle? Defending a government you hate?" asked Eliza.

"There is a lot more the knights do besides just fight, you know that Eliza...And if it came to me dying, it wouldn't be for Frog or the castle, it would be for the people of Utuk," Luca said quietly.

"I hate that you're a knight and I think ultimately you are coddled by your mothers," said Eliza.

"I guess you hate a big portion of me then...Maybe you're the one who doesn't love me," said Luca.

They swayed for a few more minutes.

"You deserve a woman who loves that part of you. And I deserve a boy who loves my free wandering spirit, and the ocean waves," said Eliza.

"I think you're right," said Luca.

The moon was beginning to fade into morning.

Let's stay like this until the sun creeps onto the horizon

because I don't believe we will find our soulmates before then.

They danced until morning, and when the sun began to peek out, they looked at each other.

"I must go," said Luca.

Eliz, without a tear in her eye, said, "Say it one more time."

"I love you, Eliza," said Luca.

"I love you, Luc," said Eliza.

They both smiled.

Quickly embraced each other with a kiss and then walked in opposite directions.

Luca was walking back home while Eliza walked away from Utuk.

———

"I called one other girl Darling, but we were not meant to be. Plus, not even one of my mothers enjoyed her company," he said with a laugh.

I looked deep into his eyes. "Do you love her now?"

Luca laid back down in the grass. "You know. I don't even know if I loved her then. I thought I knew what love was at the time, but I don't think that was what it was. She was just the first girl I saw in a different light."

"I understand," I said slowly.

"Tell me about you, Lilith, what other men have been in your life? Asked Luca.

I thought about it for a second. "I think that's a story for another day," I said.

"My arm is getting a little sore," said Luca.

"Here," I say as I move to sit up and put his head into my lap.

Luca sighs and smiles with his teeth. "This is nice...I love this... as he closes his eyes."

And "I love you," I thought to myself.

I pick up the book again and resume reading where I left off.

CHAPTER 15: DREAMS

After we had finished our chores and the sun had gone down, everyone started making their way to their hammocks. I now had my hammock in the sleeping quarters. It was underneath Luca's hammock, or instead, Luca and Carrot's hammock. I finally decided I was tired enough to go to sleep. I climbed in and wrapped myself in the soft cloth of the hammock. I looked up at the ceiling, and there was Luca with Carrot under his arm. They both looked so peaceful, but I had to admit I was a little jealous of Carrot in Luca's arms. I could hear them both snoring above me. I would listen to them snore for the rest of my life if that meant I didn't have to go back to the slave quarters and sleep in the dirt. I began to fall asleep to the rhythmic sounds of the crickets outside and Luca's breathing.

Luca's dream:

Luca looked up, and he was in the creek by the fortress, and it felt so incredibly wonderful. The sun was out, but it wasn't too warm. He ran his toes over the smooth rocks, and he watched as the little minnows swam away from him. It was a perfect day. He kept walking for what seemed like forever. He carefully walked to avoid slipping on the mossy rocks. As he finally looked out onto the horizon, he saw Lilith. She was standing in the middle of the stream, wearing a long purple dress that seemed to flow into the river at the ends. He ran to her.

"Lilith, how did you get here?" he asked.

"Well, of course, you wanted to bring me here," said Lilith with a laugh.

Luca thought hard but couldn't remember where he had been, and now Lilith was still in the purple dress, but now they were in his hammock together.

She was so close. She had never been this close to him before. He could feel his heart pumping faster.

He carefully reached out and put his hand onto the middle of her back, pulling her in even closer. She snuggled in close to his chest. He hoped she couldn't feel how fast his heart was beating.

"Can you hear my chest beating?" he asked.

Lilith replied, "No, I can't. You're dreaming, dear."

He stopped moving.

"Then how can you still be talking to me?" asked Luca.

"Because you're dreaming about me and I know you love me," said Lilith.

'That doesn't even make any sense,' mumbled Luca.

"Oh, dreams don't ever make sense," said Lilith.

Then Luca was in a field of violet.

Flowers were blooming everywhere, and Lilith was walking to him in the same purple dress. She wore a thin lavender veil over her face, adorned with a bouquet of irises.

He looked down at himself, and he was in the traditional silks for the knights.

Lilith looked at him with her piercing eyes. "Are you ready?" she asked.

"Of course! I love you more than the moon loves the stars. I never want to be apart from you. I adore you." He said it repeatedly.

And then he felt Carrot licking his face and abruptly woke up.

He sat straight up. He looked down at Lilith, and she was sound asleep. He was wondering what she was dreaming about.

Lilith's dream

"Slave girl," shouted Montgomery.

Lilith was trying to fix breakfast as fast as she could, but for some reason, the water in the pot wouldn't boil. She kept adding sticks until the flames were burning her skin, but the water was ice-cold. Just then, Montgomery started pounding towards the kitchen. Lilith threw in the remainder of the twigs and logs she had saved for the fire. The flames were so burning hot, and black smoke had filled the kitchen. Through the smoke, she could see Montgomery making her way to the oven. Montgomery shoved Lilith out of the way, reached down into the pot, and pulled out two chicks. They squawked and squealed.

"How is this even possible?" Lilith thought to herself.

The chicks were squawking.

Montgomery held the chicks in front of Lilith's face. "How do you expect me to eat these? These are chickens, not eggs."

"I swear my queen, when I put them in the pot, they were eggs," said Lilith as she lowered her head. When Lilith thought about it, she didn't remember anything about how she had gotten here or where the eggs had come from. Maybe she had put chickens into the pot, but she didn't mean to if she had.

The chicks continued squawking.

"You're making me do this, Lilith. I will have to kill them," said Montgomery.

"Please don't, Montgomery, I'll keep them." Begged Lilith.

Then they weren't in the kitchen anymore, they were in the tower of the castle, and Wilbur was standing on a ledge with a noose around his neck. The black smoke continued to fill the air.

"You never returned home, Lilith. You left them all," Said Montgomery slowly.

"I didn't leave them, I ran away from you…You wretched frog." Shouted Lilith.

"ENOUGH!" shouted Montgomery as she pushed Wilbur off the ledge.

A loud cry of anguish left Lilith's lips.

I was shaking when I awoke. To my surprise, Luca was watching me with Carrot in his arms. Are you okay? He asked.

"No, I am not. I don't think Wilbur is okay. He needs my help. I don't know how, but he needs me." I said quietly, trying not to wake the others.

"We will go there soon, I promise," Luca said, reaching down to touch my hand. "Sleep for now and gain strength.

A few miles away

Wilbur sat straight up out of a dead sleep. He looked around, and the river was flowing. The horses were sound asleep. Detrix was snoring next to him. There didn't appear to be any eyes watching him in the forest, but he felt distressed. He knew he had to get to Lilith.

BACK TO THE CASTLE: PART 6

Montgomery sat on her throne dressed in a red robe. Her face was completely white because of the amount of powder she had used to powder her face. She didn't want even one single mole to show through. She was also wearing thick red paste across her lips and cheeks. The paste was so dense that it caked around the corners of her mouth, and it seemed to string into strands when she talked.

Montgomery had sent for a painter.

Yearly, the painter would come and paint the Royal family and the guards of the castle. As a gift from the country of Climes that neighbored Utuk.

"You're painting me the way I want, correct?" asked Montgomery while she tried not to move her body.

"The painter stopped for a moment and looked at his painting and then back at Montgomery, doing my best, dear Queen." He said with a mutter.

Carac was behind the painter. "How does he normally paint you, Montgomery?" He asked.

"I normally have him paint my face and then use the slave girl for my body. But she has not returned, so I am assuming she is still looking for a husband for herself, or she has died," said Montgomery.

Carac swallowed, most days he just pretended Lilith had never existed.

"I don't think you need her, my queen, you are so much more of a woman than her anyway, she has the body of a young boy." Said Carac with the best smile he could muster.

The painter turned around and looked at Carac, rolling his eyes before returning to his painting. This went unnoticed by Carac and Montgomery.

"Let's take a break," said the painter. "We will come back to this tomorrow after my eyes have had time to umm, rest," he said after shaking his head.

Montgomery pushed herself off the throne and walked over to the painting, all while her robe had come untied and is flowed behind her.

She took one look at the painting and let out a loud shriek. "This is not what I asked for!" she screamed.

"I can only do so much, Montgomery. If you would like me to paint Lilith, then I need Lilith here. I can't dream up what she looks like." Said the painter. He had a thick accent even Montgomery herself had a hard time understanding him.

Montgomery was turning red. She turned to Carac and told the guards to find her.

Carac, who was sitting on the floor, looked up at Montgomery. "I am sorry, my queen, but with seven of the guards already looking for Detrix, that would only leave 15 here at the castle, and what if we are attacked?" He asked.

"What do you mean Detrix is missing?" Asked the Painter accusingly.

Montgomery gave a glare to Carac. "He is just a jester, he doesn't know what he is talking about," and then walked up behind Carac and pinched his ear so hard he thought it was going to fall off.

Carac let out a "welp" of pain, and Montgomery pinched tighter.

Carac had to think quickly. "Oh, I just mean that Detrix and I are playing hide and seek." Then he quickly took his hands over his eyes and started pretending to count to ten.

"He entertains the prince," Montgomery explains.

The painter looked at them both suspiciously and then walked out of the room.

Montgomery finally let go of Carac. "How could you be so stupid?" she asked. "If you slip up like that again, I will make you go back to the slave quarters where you can't talk to people,"

"I need the slave girl to finish this painting. Her time is up anyway," Spat out Montgomery.

"Send out 3 Guards, tell them I want Lilith alive and unharmed for this painting and for as far as their compensation…Well, they can have the slave girl themselves after this painting." Said Montgomery slowly.

Carac's heart was racing. "But my dear queen, you are so beautiful, you don't need her for this painting."

Montgomery looked down at him. "Are you trying to save her? You should go back to living with the goats, where she belongs?" She asked.

Carac shook his head. He had to be strong. He was getting close to a seat at the throne, which would be better than even his most excellent plan before.

Carac took his hand and ran it up Montgomery's legs. He could feel and hear her leg hairs rubbing his hand.

"All I meant is that you are so beautiful, but if you would like me to send the guards for the slave girl, I will." He said softly.

"I would, I would like that right now," as Frog pulled Carac off the floor. "Go now!"

Carac kissed her and then walked to the castle towers where the guards resided.

His heart raced with anxiety.

When he had finally finished climbing and had reached the Royal Guards, they were all sharpening their swords. The sight was menacing.

'The queen has requested that three of you look for Lilith. Lilith is currently looking for a husband for the queen. Also, she has been gone for some time. See if any of the villagers have heard of her or have found her dead. If you do find her, don't harm her." Carac announced.

"The guards looked up. That will leave very few guards here at the castle." Said Marquise.

"The queen is aware," Said Carac.

"If you return her alive and in good condition, the Queen would like to reward you all with Lilith as your slave," Carac said in a monotone.

All the men let out a cheer.

The guards were not permitted to marry anyone but were allowed to have as many partners as they liked. Carac knew of one of the few women who were sent to the guards after the king's reign was over. They didn't live long. Lilith's suffering would be short-lived. The guards had no self-control when it came to the presents they received from the queen.

CHAPTER 16: KNIGHTHOOD

Detrix bent down to pick up a small, smooth stone from the river. The stone was white and had been worn down by years of rushing water over its edges.

"Look, Wilbur, a diamond!" Shouted Detrix.

Wilbur took the rock in his hand and rubbed it with his thumb and finger. He didn't have the heart to tell him it was just a rock. "Oh, this is a nice diamond," said Wilbur.

"I am going to give it to Lilith when we find her!" Proclaimed Detrix.

"I am sure she will love it," said Wilbur with a smile.

They walked for a few more moments.

"How much longer do we have to walk through the river? My feet are tired," said Detrix.

"For the day. I know that along this way are the knights of Utuk. The Knights have taken an oath to care for the people of Utuk, including the slaves. I pray they remain loyal to the people as they were when I was a young man. I pray they aren't loyal to Montgomery," he said to Detrix.

I was sitting in my hammock, petting Carrot while reading my book, when Ebba came to my hammock.

Carrot had grown quite fond of me, and I had grown quite fond of her.

"Lilith, we, the sisters, have decided it is time for your fitting," Ebba said.

I was aware of the deeply rooted importance of this event. I grabbed her wrist. "Are you sure I am ready?" I asked.

She put her hand over mine and looked at me with her pure green eyes. "Yes, it is time. You have shown your loyalty."

She led me to the armory. Red candles lined the room. All the knights were dressed in elaborate traditional knights' garb, each with a distinct color, and a flail was placed in the center of the room. My flail was placed in the center of the room.

All the women sat in a circle, their heads bent down and their hands on the floor, in silence. Ebba quickly took her place in the circle. I noticed Luca was wearing his battle sword.

I took my place in the circle. As I placed my hands on the floor, I looked up and there was Luca across the circle, smiling at me. I smiled back but suddenly stopped. This was a time of importance.

After I had taken my place, all the women began to hum and started beating the floor with their palms in unison. I could feel the vibrations throughout my whole body. On the third beat, I stood up and took off all my clothes except for my underclothes. It was then that Luca broke from the circle and stood up. He handed me a purple knight's uniform. It was mine. It had to be. It was a rich, deep purple. It was so beautiful I almost didn't want to ruin it by wearing it. Luca was in the center of the circle, he handed me a pair of black pants on his knees. This was the first part of" the fitting." Everyone had the same black pants. I stepped into the pants, and Luca, still on his knees, tied the front of them behind me, and then he tied the back of the pants in front of me with the long ribbons attached.

I saw his hands shaking slightly. He must have been nervous. Then he stood up and helped me put on the deep purple jacket. It was also made with silk and felt so crisp against my skin. It had the crest of the Knights on the back, and there was one ribbon to tie on the inside of the jacket and one on the outside. Then Luca motioned for us both to sit down, and he brushed my hair with a goat-hair brush until it was silky soft, then tied my hair back with a strip of leather. He then took his place back into the circle, placed his hand on the floor, and began beating the floor in unison with the others.

I picked up the Flail and stopped my foot loudly on the ground to let the others know I was ready, and everyone grew silent.

And then I loudly proclaimed. "I vow to honor the people of Utuk until my dying breath, and I vow loyalty to my fellow knights!" I said with a shout!

They all got up and grabbed torches from the fire, and then we walked outside.

There was a pig's head attached to a stick, and in the center of the pig's head was a word carved into it: "Montgomery."

They all began chanting. Just then, Luca poured oil over my flail and then put his torch to the spikes.

I let my flail fly into the center of the pig's head. Time seemed to slow down for a moment, and then the whole head burst into flames.

Everyone began cheering. I stood there for a moment. Staring into the dark at the flames.

Luca lifted me onto his shoulders, and everyone began running in circles around us. Singing and cheering

I threw a fist into the air and let out a scream.

The knights had chosen me to protect the Kingdom, to protect the people, to live with them, to be one of them, but it wasn't going to be easy. I had a mission. I had a mission to kill Montgomery.

Wilbur stopped in his tracks and motioned to Detrix to quiet the horses.

He held a hand to his ear and listened.

"Do you hear that, Detrix? That's a warrior's chant. That means we must be close," Wilbur whispered.

Detrix just continued patting the horses for a moment. "They sound scary," said Detrix.

"Oh, they are," said Wilbur with a grin.

CHAPTER 17: RUNAWAY

"Look, there it is," said Wilbur to Detrix. The sun had just began to creep above the horizon and shine light on the fortress.

"It looks kind of like a small castle," said Detrix, who was still holding both horses' reins.

"It has a similar design to the castle, so the people of Utuk will be able to recognize it as their own. The same man designed it," said Wilbur.

Detrix started walking out of the woods.

"Stop! Detrix, we don't want them to be aware of our presence until we know they are friendly. I haven't been out of those castle walls in your lifetime. The knights might not be as honorable as they were before. Now tie the horses up by the water out of the sight of the knights," said Wilbur in a hushed whisper.

Detrix did so and then sat down next to Wilbur in the leaves.

They covered their faces and hair with mud and leaves to blend into the forest floor. They took branches and wove them into their hair.

Wilbur moved slowly onto his stomach, so his head wasn't as visible, and Detrix followed.

"Now we wait," said Wilbur softly.

When I awoke, Carrot was in my hammock underneath my arm. She must have hopped into my arms during the night. She had started alternating sleeping with Luca and I.

Luca jumped down from his hammock.

"Good morning, my beautiful knight," he said as he took a piece of my hair and stroked it behind my ear.

"I'm going to take Saturn out for a run if that's okay. He looked anxious yesterday," said Luca.

"Was Saturn anxious, or did you just want to ride Saturn?" I asked with a smile.

Luca rolled his eyes. "Okay, so maybe I have been wanting to take him out since you got here." Said Luca.

"Take him. I am sure he would love to get out of the stables for a bit. Carrot and I will be back here when you get back." I said as I snuggle deep into my hammock with Carrot.

———

Detrix shook Wilbur awake. "That's one of the knights."

Wilbur narrowed his eyes. It was. He looked like a strapping young knight. He stood taller than both. He had dark wavy hair that reached his ears, and he walked with a slight skip. He must have been in a hurry, so he walked into the stables and disappeared.

Then out of the stables he walked with a black horse.

Wilbur's jaw dropped. "That's Saturn!" He said, turning to Detrix in a loud whisper.

"Do you think Lilith is in there?" Detrix asked.

Wilbur's heart started pumping so fast. He couldn't imagine

Lilith willingly letting someone else ride Saturn. Saturn was the pride of the entire castle in Wilbur's mind. He worried Lilith was being held captive there. "By the scallywag that just took Saturn off into the land like it was his. How dare he?" Wilbur thought to himself. He couldn't believe what had happened.

"Detrix, later, when we are ready, we will attack this fortress and save Lilith," Wilbur assured him.

"This whole Kingdom has gone to pot," said Wilbur, shaking his head.

Luca pulled his favorite riding blanket from the stables. It was green and featured gold thread through the stitching, as well as the royal crest of the knight on both sides. He then took Saturn and led him out into the grass. Saturn's nostrils were flaring in excitement. Once he had finished putting the blanket on Saturn, he jumped up onto the horse. Instantly, Saturn was running. Luca felt like he was on top of the world. He let go of the horse with both hands, threw them up in the air, and let out a yell.

A few minutes went by, and Saturn's gallop turned into a trot. Luca could still feel a surge of adrenaline pumping through his veins. He started slowly, guiding Saturn in the direction of the closest village. This was the first time he had been by himself in a while. He took a deep breath in. Before Lilith, he used to take rides like this all the time, but now he felt lonely without her.

Luca decided to go into one of the villages and get Lilith

a present. When he arrived, everything looked normal. He jumped off Saturn and tied him to a post. Children were playing while their parents were working. An old couple sat working on candles together. Everyone looked pleased. Luca made his way to the center of the village, where the blacksmith was hammering away on something he was making. Then Luca saw a poster. It read.

From Royal Order of the Queen:

Runaway Slave Girl

Rewarded: ten bags of grain from the royal armory

Luca ripped the poster off the wall. "What is this?" Luca demanded from the Blacksmith.

"Oh, hello there, Luca," I didn't see you replied the blacksmith nonchalantly.

Luca was still holding the poster.

"Oh, that?" asked the blacksmith as he took the poster out of Luca's hands and nailed it back on the wall. "The royal guards came by the villages and said if we can find this runaway slave, we will be rewarded with 10 bags of grain," said the blacksmith excitedly. "That would be enough food for the village for the entire winter."

Luca was dumbfounded. "It was a matter of time before they checked the knight's fortress. They could be there right now." Luca thought.

"What's wrong, boy? Going all sympathetic on some slave girl? They have a better life at the castle than we do," The

Blacksmith said.

Luca knew the blacksmith was already a little suspicious of his reaction, so he had to cover.

"Mind if I take this poster to the knights to see if they have seen her? We move all over the kingdom. She might have joined up with the Nomads. I am seeing them soon for a silk order," he said calmly.

"Now don't you be taking the reward all for yourself! You want the reward for yourself," said the blacksmith.

"Don't worry," Luca laughed nervously. He had to get back to Lilith quickly.

BACK TO THE CASTLE: PART 7

Carac slowly picked up all of Montgomery's clothes off the cold marble floor from the evening before.

Montgomery sat on her throne, wearing only a peacock feather boa and her undergarments. She was finishing off a cake on a gold platter from the night before. A piece of the icing fell from her mouth and onto her body. She stopped chewing for a moment and licked off the icing.

Carac saw the guards walk by in the halls. He suddenly felt a surge of shame. "What had he become? Was he any better than the whores that walked the streets? He didn't have a single friend in this world. His skin and hair were covered in grease since living in the castle. His diet only consisted of grain and milk. His stomach cast over his pants." His thoughts ran wild. He bent down to put on his shirt to cover himself.

Montgomery looked up from her cake. "Carac, don't wear your shirt. You look better like that to me," and then she continued eating.

Carac took off his shirt slowly and looked directly at Montgomery.

She placed the platter on the floor, pushed herself off her throne, took her boa in both hands, wrapped it around Carac's body, and pulled him close to her. Then she bent down close to his ear and said, "Ready to play again, puppet?"

----

2 years ago

It was a chilly winter night. Lilith and Carac had started a small fire in their quarters with the leftover twigs from Montgomery's fireplace. Wilbur was on duty to keep the fire going in the castle all night, so it was just the two of them in the quarters.

Lilith was shaking while she slept, so Carac went to the stables and got them two riding blankets. He placed them both over Lilith and got under the blankets himself behind her. Lilith turned around and their faces were almost touching.

"You must take these back, Carac. If they catch us with these, we could be punished," Lilith said, shivering.

"Don't worry, neither Frog nor her guards will be coming out of their warm castle to check on us. We will take them back in the morning," said Carac.

That put Lilith's mind at ease.

She snuggled her head into his chest. "You make me feel safe," she said before she drifted off again.

Carac took his arms and wrapped them around her.

Just before Montgomery was going to go any further, the guards interrupted.

"My highness, we believe we have located the runaway slaves and your brother. We have received word from a few of the villages that they are all hiding around the knight's fortress," one said in a loud voice.

Montgomery pushed Carac away. "If you know where they are, why aren't they back where they belong?" she asked.

He swallowed. "We don't know exactly where they are, and that is just some hearsay from a few of the villages."

"Well then, figure it out," Montgomery shouted. "Any man

in the Kingdom of Utuk would be thrilled to be a guard for the royal kingdom. Don't you believe any one of you can't be replaced by tomorrow?" She warned.

He bowed his head and exited the room.

Carac suddenly had an idea. "My dearest queen, put me in charge of those imbeciles that keep wasting our precious moments together," he whispered in her ear.

If he became a guard, he would hold royal status and would oversee everyone except the Queen. He would be the second-in-command over the Kingdom.

Montgomery looked down upon him. "How do I know you will be loyal to me?" asked Montgomery.

Carac kissed her neck. "How could you even question my loyalty? I am loyal only to you." He reassured her.

Montgomery let out a laugh. "Do you think I am that stupid? Of course, you're going to say that, but can you prove it? How could you prove your loyalty to me?"

Carac got on his knees and started kissing her feet.

Montgomery pulled him up off the floor. "You know how you could prove yourself to me? Bring me Lilith."

Carac looked at her for a moment in panic. "How about I bring your fool brother instead? Lilith isn't that important."

"I know she once was important to you, though…" Montgomery said under her breath. "You have been calling out her name in your sleep."

"Bring me Lilith, and your loyalty will be proven," said Montgomery.

"Yes, my queen. I shall bring her to you." Said Carac without hesitation.

Montgomery took her robe out of Carac's hands and tied it around her waist.

"I won't send you off without training, dear Carac. To become a Head Guardsman, you must undergo training before the capture. Tomorrow will be your first swordsman lesson. Go to the King's quarters and try my father's battle equipment." She commanded.

Carac was giddy with excitement; this wasn't all for a loss.

He went immediately to the King's quarters on the other side of the castle.

What Montgomery didn't know is that he already knew the King's fencing equipment fit him.

———

A year and a half ago

"Carac! Stop it!" Said Lilith in a loud whisper.

Lilith and Carac oversaw dusting the entire King's quarters.

"Frog is going to catch you in her father's clothes," said Lilith.

Carac laughed. "Frog is still eating breakfast. The guards are gone collecting taxes. No one is going to catch us." He said as he slipped on the Kings' silver helmet.

Lilith continued dusting hurriedly.

"Look, I'm the King of Utuk!" shouted Carac as he jumped onto the bed.

"Get off of there," scolded Lilith, but she couldn't help but smile.

Carac proudly marched around the room, as if he were telling people what to do.

Then he walked over to Lilith and handed her a tiara that had once belonged to the former Queen.

"My Queen, shall I have this dance?" asked Carac.

Lilith rolled her eyes and placed the duster on the bed. "Okay, but only for a minute." She said quickly.

She took his hand, and they swayed back and forth while Carac hummed a tune.

It was just for a moment, but they truly felt like the real King and Queen of Utuk.

CHAPTER 18: MARQUISE

Carrot jumped out of my hammock and started barking at me with her little barks. I rolled over and looked at her. "Does this mean I have to get out of bed?" I ask her. She barked twice, as if to say, "You've been in bed long enough," and was telling me she wanted me to get up. I slipped on my pants and shirt right before Luca slammed the door open and shut it behind him. This startled me quite a bit. He leaned up against the wall, breathing deeply like he had been running.

"You. Can't. Leave. The. Fortress. The guards have put a bounty on your head," said Luca, panting for air.

"What?" I asked him, perplexed.

He hands me a sheet of paper. It read:

From Royal Order of the Queen:
Runaway Slave Girl

Rewarded: ten bags of grain from the royal armory

It made my stomach turn. I instantly ripped the paper and threw it into the fire out of pure frustration.

Luca had caught his breath. You should stay inside until this blows over. In a few weeks, people will have forgotten about this.

"Let them come," I said calmly.

Luca looked at me like I had lost my mind.

"I know exactly which guard will come to collect me," I said.

"What does that matter?" asked Luca.

In the not-so-distant past before the King's passing.

Marquise stood in the doorway of the servant's quarters. His thoughts of Felix were overwhelming.

"Hello, Lilith," he said as he twisted his moustache.

"What do you want?" asked Lilith.

"Let's not play games, little one," he said as he walked closer into the quarters.

He reached out with his long fingers and picked up a piece of Lilith's hair. He took a deep breath in. His breathing reminded Lilith of the dogs around a pig carcass after a feast.

"You're not going to touch me," Said Lilith through gritted teeth.

This angered Marquise, and he shoved her down. She reminded him so much of Felix.

Lilith gave him a defiant look. "If you lay one more finger on me, I will tell the King, and your comrades will know what a rat you truly are. I am giving you one last chance, Marquise," She warned.

"Trust me, the King has done much worse than this." Said Marquise. He grabbed Lilith's hair in a clump like he was going to take her somewhere.

"I am not denying that fact; however, I know I am the King's favorite for whatever reason." Said Lilith

"We will see about that," Marquise whispered in her ear, and then he started trying to rip her dress off her shoulders.

Then she let out a blood-curdling scream. Marquise tried to quiet her, but his attempts were unsuccessful.

Suddenly, the King himself appeared in the doorway. What he saw deeply bothered him. His headguard was pulling Lilith's dress off.

"Get off of her!" Shouted the King in his booming voice.

He ran into the quarters and pulled Marquise off Lilith. He held him up by the collar of his shirt. "You, Marquise, have wronged me for the last time." He pulled a dagger from his belt.

Marquise was now yelling at the King to stop. "Felix, not after everything we have been through. This is just your servant girl. You know your father always had his way with his servants." He almost threatened.

Felix slapped him across the face. "When have I <u>ever</u> been like my father?"

The king looked down at him. "Stop it, you fool. You know everyone has consequences for their actions," he shouted.

Marquise stopped shouting and exited the servant's quarters, obediently kneeling at the King's feet.

"Spread your fingers, Marquise," Felix boomed.

Marquise laid his hand on the ground and spread out all his fingers. His body shaking.

"Come here, Lilith," shouted the King. Lilith did so obediently.

The king handed her his sword with a smirk on his face "a present for you."

Lilith knew the sword wasn't the present.

She drew back the dagger. "I want you to watch Marquise don't hide your face," she shouted.

Marquise begged. "Please no, I will be ruined."

Lilith slowly cut off his pinky fingers. First, to the Right, then the left. She could feel his bones cracking through the sword.

The king let out a deep laugh that could be heard across the entire Kingdom.

Marquise stood up with blood pouring down his arms. "My life is ruined," he said while sobbing. "I didn't even bite into her fruit."

In the Kingdom of Utuk, any sexual crime was punished by removing both pinky fingers. So, they would feel shame every time someone looked at their hands until they died.

Lilith thought she would feel remorse or guilt in this moment, but what she felt instead was a surge of adrenaline.

"Leave our site," she shouted.

"One day I will get my revenge upon you," Marquise said through sobs, then he ran away in shame.

Montgomery watched from her room. She hated her father. His loyalty to the servants annoyed her. "Now he had lost his best guardsman and his protector," she thought. Montgomery smiled because she knew this would all be part of his downfall.

Back to the Knights

"Marquise will be coming for me he will not want the grain for himself, but the revenge." I warned

"Do you think the King did worse than Marquise was planning to do to you?" asked Luca.

"I don't know…" I said as my voice trailed off.

"I know he killed many people, but I always wondered if it was for the right reasons," I said.

"Regardless, Marquise is a terrible man," Luca added.

"If given the opportunity, I want to finish Marquise," I said.

CHAPTER 19: MIDNIGHT

The sky had grown dark, and the moon had come out to shine. The grass was wet with rain, and I could hear the frogs by the river singing their love songs. I sat outside, leaning against the fortress. I should have been asleep, but my mind was filled with so many thoughts. I heard the door open next to me. It was Luca.

"Why aren't you asleep?" he asked.

"I have a lot on my mind," I said.

He sat down in front of me and grabbed my hand. Rubbing his this thumb on mine,

Even the lightest touch from Luca made me want to melt into him.

Luca looked up into the sky.

"Did you know that all the stars have names?" asked Luca.

"I did. The king used to take me out of the castle after everyone had gone to bed and show me all the stars and their names." I told him.

"Today was my birthday," I said.

Luca stopped what he was doing. "Why didn't you say so?" And he reached down into his pocket and pulled out a small leather necklace with a pendant in the shape of a circle.

"Is this for me?" I asked.

"Yes! I got this for you quite a while ago. I have been waiting for the right time to give it to you," he said with his best smile.

I took the necklace and put it around my neck.

---

10 years ago

The king walked into Montgomery's quarters. He slowly crept until he found Lilith on the floor. He slowly picked her up, trying not to wake her.

With Lilith in his arms, he slowly crept out of the room.

She opened her eyes. "Where are we going?" She asked quietly.

He bent his neck down so he could whisper in her ear. 'I'm taking you somewhere for today is your Birthday!" He said in a whisper.

"It's my birthday, Lilith," asked excitedly.

"Yes, child." Said the King.

Once they were outside of the castle, the King put Lilith down on the ground and reached into his pocket and pulled out a small ring with a red ruby in the center and extended his hand out to Lilith, "For you," just don't let the princess see it." Said the King quietly.

Lilith put the ring on, but it was too large for her tiny finger, and it fell off.

The king laughed and pulled a string from his jacket, wrapping it around the bottom.

"Try now," the king urged.

Lilith put it on. "It fits perfectly but, Felix, if I can't wear my ring in front of the Princess, when will I wear it?" asked Lilith.

The king took a deep breath and seemed to wipe away a tear. "One day, Lilith, I hope you can wear it every day, but for now you will need to keep it under your mattress, and maybe when that day comes, you won't need the string to wear it, you can wear it openly." Said the King.

Lilith nodded. It was beautiful; the moonlight seemed to shine off the ring.

"Lilith, I want to take you somewhere special for your birthday, but we have to be back by sunup, so we must hurry." Said the King.

They quickly ran to the stables and climbed on the King's stallion. "Okay, Lilith, close your eyes." Said the King

Lilith did so without question.

After a while, Felix told her to open her eyes. What she saw took her breath away. They were on the highest part of the Kingdom. The moon was shining so brightly that they could see the entire kingdom. Lilith had never seen anything like it.

Felix jumped off his horse and carried Lilith down with him.

"Can we stay here for a little while?" asked Lilith.

"I thought you might ask that," said the king, and he pulled two candy sticks and two blankets from his satchel.

They sat on the hillside for a while, eating their candy.

"Why did you take me here?" asked Lilith.

"I thought you might like it here." Said the king.

"I once had a friend. Her favorite place was here." Said the king.

―――

Back to the Knights

"This is beautiful, Luca. It fits me perfectly," I said as I placed it around my neck.

I put my hand on Luca's jaw around his ear, leaned in, and kissed him.

Luca turned red. "You didn't have to do that." He said nervously.

"Oh. But I wanted to." I said with a smile.

Luca was so big and strong, I couldn't imagine a little kiss could take him down.

I moved close to Luca and placed both my arms on his shoulders. I could feel his hair on the tops of my arms. He slid one hand around my waist and the other in the middle of my back.

He stopped and stared into my eyes. "I don't think we have ever been this close before." He said softly into my ear.

Then he gently took his hand into my hair and grabbed a handful. My hair fell back like the water falling off a duck's tail. He took my hair and pulled my head back and began kissing my neck. He grasped me tightly.

It was my turn to be taken off guard now. I couldn't help but let a moan of satisfaction escape my lips and into the night. I grabbed Luca tighter and pulled him into my arms.

My fingernails grazed his back slowly.

When we were finally looking at each other again, I leaned and kissed him like I had never kissed anyone before.

He rolled back, and now I was on top of him. Our lips were about to touch again when I heard a bark, and we both stopped.

It was Carrot. Luca turned and looked at her. "Carrot, go inside, you silly dog. How did you get out?"

I laughed. "Well, if we woke Carrot up, we should probably go back to bed before we awaken anyone else."

Luca leaned up. "If you insist," he said as he kissed my forehead.

BACK TO THE CASTLE: PART 8

Marquise drew his sword and looked at his reflection in its blade.

Carac entered the dojo.

"Montgomery would like for you to start training me in the arts," Carac announced to Marquise.

Marquise drew his blade back into its sheath. "I am aware."

"When do we start training? It needs to be soon," Carac insisted with urgency.

"Carac, you have impressed the queen with your lover boy antics, and I am pleased with you keeping Montgomery entertained. However, you should know that these guards have given up everything since boyhood to be here. I will train you to the best of my abilities over the next few days, but they are the best fighters in all the land. Men run away when they see them walking down the street. I could spend my lifetime training you, and it wouldn't compare to them." Marquise fixed his mustache between his two fingers. I can teach you how to avoid being killed in the next few days.

Carac considered for a moment. "What am I to tell the queen then?"

"You're going to tell her you trained with me. When the real action happens, you'll stay out of my way. When we get the slave girl and the prince, we will hand them over to you before we cross the castle gates," Marquise said blatantly.

Carac was more than pleased with the answer and began trying on the guards' uniforms.

James overheard the conversation from the back of the dojo. He seethed with anger. He had spent his life hoping Montgomery would glance his way.

Her beauty entranced him, how she carried herself, so indulgent and unapologetic. He would give his life to love her the way she deserved to be loved.

This scoundrel had made his way into her life, and now he would have to capture the slave girl and her brother and hand them over to this Carac. He didn't know if he could stand it.

He walked over to Marquise.

"You can't be serious!" He whispered.

Marquise looked at James with pity. "You know that's the only way."

"I haven't spent my life training for this slave to take the credit!" He said louder than he should have. All I do is think about her day and night," James pleaded.

Marquise pulled some money from his jacket. "Go to the brothel and satisfy whatever needs you may have."

"That's not working anymore," James countered.

Marquise motioned for him to lower his voice. "That is what will make Montgomery happy," he said.

He grabbed James' shoulder. "You can't get caught up in feelings, James, you can't live your life thinking you will catch her eye. It's forbidden. We are here to protect her and nothing else."

---

20 Years prior

Prince Felix drew his sword and sliced through the air back and forth. He was practicing his fencing. It was his absolute favorite sport, and he spent most of his time doing.

Marquise was watching him from a far enough distance that he could watch Felix, but Felix couldn't see him. He was a guardsman in training, and it was his duty to make sure the prince stayed safe.

"I know you're there, Marquise!" shouted the prince as he continued to make slices through the air. "I can feel you watching me."

Marquise stepped out of the shadows. "I thought I was going to sneak up on you this time." He said with a chuckle.

The prince put his sword in his sheath.

"Let's practice our fencing together," the prince said excitedly.

"Aren't you supposed to be practicing your Geometry or Astrology or something like that?" asked Marquise.

"Are you scared that I would be better with a sword than you?" Asked Felix.

This angered Marquise. "No, I am just pointing out that Kings don't do their fighting. That is what the guardsmen are for."

"Well, when I am king, I will march into any battle with my men," declared Felix.

"Fine, then this time tomorrow we will both be prepared to have a duel with our swords. The winner will be declared the best fencer of Utuk," said marquise.

The young men gathered all their friends around the courtyard the next day.

Both were dressed in the finest fencing uniforms in the Kingdom of Utuk. They were identical so that it would be an actual test of each other's skills.

The prince stood with his sword in his sheath, calmly breathing deeply in and out, mentally preparing himself for the spar.

Marquise took a large bite out of a green apple he had picked from the orchards. He seemed like he didn't have a care in the world.

One of the boy's friends took a stance in the middle. "We have all gathered here today to declare the best fencer of Utuk!" The small group that had gathered let out a cheer.

"To my right we have Prince Felix and to my Left we have Marquise guard in training."

"Are you ready, gentlemen?" He asked. Both Felix and Marquise nodded.

The young men drew their swords. They both charged at each other, and you could hear a clink as the swords collided.

They spared for a few minutes. Each time you thought the spar was over, one of them would gracefully step out of the way of the swords.

They fought for several minutes, and then out of nowhere, Prince Felix smiled and winked at Marquise. Marquise was taken off guard, and that was all Felix needed. He struck the sword from Marquise's hand. Marquise was left feeling naked and ashamed. The pampered Prince had beaten him.

Felix drew his sword back into his belt and took a bow while the small group of friends cheered.

Marquise took his sword from the ground with the small amount of dignity he could muster and started to walk away.

Felix grabbed his shoulder and stopped him. "You, my sir, will be my head guardsman as you have fought very well today."

Marquise had trained his whole life in hopes he would be chosen for this position.

"But, sir, why would you choose me? You could defeat me yourself?" Asked Marquise

Felix grabbed his shoulder. "You, my Guardsmen, are the 2nd best fencer in the Kingdom of Utuk, and it would be an honor for you to be my right hand."

Marquise beamed with Pride. He took a bow in front of the King.

CHAPTER 20: KNIGHTS OF BASIL

I watched Ebba scoop the last cup of flour from the barrel for everyone's breakfast. The others were all laughing as if nothing was out of the ordinary. We locked eyes at that moment, and she motioned for me to come closer.

"Don't say anything to the others. Let them have this meal without worrying about the next," She whispered.

I nodded to avoid drawing attention to ourselves.

"The knights were fortunate to have flour for this long. We always had the meat from the animal hunts, but even with all the protein, we still risked starving to death without the grain. The queen has taken so much from the people. We tried giving out flour and grains when we could, but we have given so much that we have none left for ourselves. Ebba's usual happy face had faded.

Luca had been teaching me about everyday life in Utuk over the last few weeks. After learning that Montgomery would charge the people of Utuk a tax, and if they didn't have the money for the taxes, they would "kindly" take their food as a replacement. It made so much sense when he told me. I had no idea Montgomery was also taking the little food the people had. The guards would come marching in with Wagons of food, but I had no idea where it came from. I remembered Montgomery would have the guards collect it and let them feast with her on these days in celebration. It was one of the ways she kept the guard so close to her. They were continuously fed well.

After we had finished our meal and cleaned up the mess, I went to talk to Ebba, who was practicing throwing Axes into our target. She looked up long enough to nod at me to let me know she knew I was there.

I picked up an Axe and began throwing with her. I had gotten even better at precision since the ceremony.

"We have till tomorrow to avoid starving to death," Ebba says jokingly, but her smile quickly fades away.

"I think I have a temporary solution," I said.

Ebba was aiming to take Axe to the target, but when she heard my words, she stopped and looked at me. "What would that be?" she asked.

"We could sneak into the castle and take just one barrel of grain. We could sneak right under Montgomery's nose," I said with confidence.

"It would be killing two birds with one stone. I must return soon to rescue my friends. We could do it all in 1 night," I said.

It all seemed quite simple when I discussed it with Ebba, but it would require a lot of planning, and what would I tell Carac? Would I mention Luca to him? Carac would be so thrilled to be freed, he wouldn't even care enough about me to say goodbye. He would just run off to his village with his family, which he always talked about.

Ebba spoke up, drawing me out of my thoughts. "I don't see any other option," she said grimly and threw another Ax.

Wilbur crept through the forest floor on his stomach with his hand-forged weapons tied to his back. He had mud all over his face and branches sticking through his clothes. He truly looked like a part of the forest. Wilbur was a true master of camouflage. Detrix wasn't far behind him. They crept until they were just shy of earshot of the knight's fortress. Wilbur motioned for Detrix to stop moving. They both stopped and slowly looked at the fortress.

They could see two women throwing Axes.

Wilbur whispered to Detrix, "I can't believe that they have women caught up in their sick games."

Detrix squinted his eyes hard. "Do you think that one could be Lilith?" he asked as he pointed.

Wilbur quickly pushed Detrix's arm down so it couldn't be seen.

"No, no, it couldn't be," said Wilbur, and he looked again. "My Goodness gracious, I think it is our Lilith."

"Do you think she is a knight?" asked Detrix.

"She has only been gone for a month, but I guess it's possible," Wilbur said with astonishment.

"You know, Detrix, I used to be a knight. That was when I was known as Knight Wilburn of Basil," he said with pride.

―――

20 years prior

Wilburn drew his sword from his belt and began slicing through the hay targets in front of him. Each one was easier than the last. You could smell the fresh hay falling through the air. All the other Knights sat back and leaned up against a giant tree nearby. Once Wilburn had sliced through all the targets, he quickly drew his sword from his belt and took a bow to his comrades. They all cheered.

One older man got up. "Well, my goodness gracious, Wilburn, you might be the best swordsman in Basil."

Wilbur just beamed with pride and grasped the man's hand in a sign of friendship.

Later in the day. Wilburn drew his sword again and looked at his reflection in the shining metal. He took the hem of his shirt and started to polish it as if it weren't already glowing.

As he polished it, he could see his beautiful bride behind him looking at his eyes. She had the most gorgeous eyes that the Kingdom of Basil had ever seen.

"When you dream at night, are your hands running down my body or are they running down your sword?" she asked with a laugh.

Wilburn took his sword into its sheath onto his belt and grabbed Kato by her hips and pulled her onto himself.

She threw her arms around him, and they began kissing passionately.

Wilburn stopped for a moment and sat her down, stroking her auburn hair behind her ear. "There is nothing I could ever love more than you. Not even in one thousand lifetimes."

"What if I told you I was with child"? she asked.

Back to the fortress

"Wilbur! That is Lilith! Let's tell her we are here," Said Detrix hurriedly.

But Wilbur took his hand in front of Detrix's mouth. "Not so quickly, boy. We need to find a time when Lilith is alone. We don't know how friendly they are. I hope they are, but you never know for sure, and judging from their target practice over there, they don't seem like a group to be messed with. "

BACK AT THE CASTLE: PART 9

"**L**et's get personal today," said Marquise to his guardsmen in the dojo.

Carac looked at him with question.

"Let's focus only on our hand to hand combat, no other weapons today, Carac go get a mat from Felix's room," Marquise annouced.

Carac began scampering up to the King's room.

"Just don't mess anything up in there. I want it like the King left it," Marquise demanded.

Carac bowed as a sign of respect for his teacher and then went off to find the mat that Marquise had spoken of. He came to the late King's quarters. The room was huge, and since the King passed, Montgomery had filled it with copious amounts of items she didn't have any use for. After rummaging for quite a long time, he found the mat, but it was covered in old books. He carelessly threw the books under the bed, hoping to get to the mat as fast as he could. It was then that he spotted a painted picture of Lilith and Montgomery as children. It was a strange sight to see them both together. He wondered what they were both like as little girls. Did they play together? Was Montgomery awful then? He didn't let the thoughts linger long before throwing the painting under the bed. He finally made it back into the dojo.

"Took you long enough," scoffed James.

Marquise glared at James and then began speaking, "I once met a pirate who sailed to a small place where they practiced the art of Judo," Said Marquise as he sat down.

"Judo? Asked Carac

"Yes, the pirate told me it means *the gentle way*," said Marquise.

"No disrespect intended, but I want to be the best warrior there is. I don't want to be gentle," Said Carac.

"Oh, just wait, I think you will change your mind," said

Marquise.

Marquise took Carac's hands and placed them on his shirt collar. Then, Marquise grabbed the collar of Carac's shirt and, with his other hand, grabbed the bottom of the sleeve.

Carac, still looking puzzled, asked, "What are we going to do? dance?" He laughed.

"Now you're getting it," shouted Marquise. He quickly turned and grabbed Carac around his waist, lifting him into the air and then down onto the mat.

Carac was shocked once again by Marquise. He was much taller and stronger than Marquise, and he couldn't believe what had just happened. "How? How did you get my feet off the ground so quickly? I felt like I had such a strong stance," he said.

Marquise just smiled, "Now it's your turn".

Across the room, a few guardsmen leaned against the wall, watching as Marquise and Carac practiced hand-to-hand combat skills. Marquise said it was important that everyone watch and learn, but the guardsmen were bored and began talking to one another.

One of the guardsmen turned to the group, "Did you know that Carac sleeps in Frog's quarters now like a pet pussy cat," as he let out a laugh. "I can't imagine."

"If I could only be him," James says with a sigh.

The entire group stops what they are doing and looks at him, shocked.

"How could you not be completely enamored with her beauty? The way her body curves. The way she dresses is so provocative. The way she talks to me. How does she dominate every conversation to her liking? That woman indulges herself in every way she can. I can't even be in the same room with her…. Without… My trousers tightening," and he trails off.

The other men look at each other and shake their heads in unison.

One man spoke up, "You know you don't have to pretend with us, right? There is a reason <u>everyone</u> in the kingdom calls her a frog."

"Oh, trust me, I'm not. I would give up every girl in Utuk to be with her just for one night." He says quickly.

Just then, Montgomery walks into the room to watch Carac and Marquise grapple. She had a chalice of wine and appeared to be eating boiled eggs from her pocket. She was scandalously dressed in only a thin robe tied around her waist.

"Just look at her. I daydream that she will walk in to give me my orders one day, and her robe will be blown off with the wind." James said, almost drooling like a dog.

"You need to visit with us at the brothel tomorrow. They got a very well-fed woman down there." Said one of the men.

John walked away in frustration. He was going with them, but there wasn't a woman alive who compared to his dearest

Montgomery. It wasn't just the way she looked; he was hungry for only her.

On the other side of the room, Montgomery heard her name and looked up. She could see the young guardsmen. The young man met Montgomery's gaze for a moment and then quickly looked away. She narrowed her eyes to make out which one he was. It was James. He was younger than most of the guards and by far the smallest. He had tiny wrists and hands that looked frail to the touch. He had red hair that was greasy and always in his light eyes. She thought he was the ugliest of the guardsmen. Montgomery was always on the prowl for a new puppet. When one became too boring, she would get a new one, but James would certainly not be on her list.

Marquise sat on Carac boasting that he had once again won the match. Carac tapped his hand twice on the ground to let Marquise know that it was time for Marquise to let him go.

Both men were covered in sweat, and the room felt dewy in the air.

Carac wiped the sweat off his brow and blew a kiss to Montgomery.

Frog smiled back and took another nibble of her egg.

CHAPTER 21: MEMORIES

I decided to tell Luca about the plan Ebba, and I had discussed earlier. I wasn't sure how he would react. I was scared he would be mad at me for making such big plans without his input. I was also afraid to tell him about my plans to rescue my friends, especially Carac.

When I found Luca, he was polishing his sword with his shirt. His bulging shoulders almost popped out of his back. I had to take a breath before approaching him.

"Luca, I need to talk to you about something," I said.

He looked up at me, slid his sword into its sheath, and then pulled me onto his lap, where we were facing each other.

I rolled my eyes at him. "We can't have a conversation this close," I said with a laugh.

"Oh, of course we can," he said as he kissed me quickly.

"I don't think we will be doing much talking this way," I said.

"If you insist," he said with a smile and leans himself up against the tree.

"I have decided to go back to the castle and steal a barrel of wheat from Montgomery, and I must rescue my friends before it's too late," I said sheepishly, a little scared to look at his reaction.

Luca drew his hand to his chin as if he were thinking. It was so quiet I could hear his fingers run against the grain of his hair on his face.

"That could be dangerous," He seemed worried.

"I know, but I don't see another way of freeing my friends and getting grain," I added.

He took a deep breath. "You have spoken of your friend Wilbur.

And how he is like your father in ways. But who is your other friend? You haven't talked much about his specifics?" Luca asked.

It was a fair question, but I didn't like discussing it with Luca, fearing he would be filled with jealousy and wouldn't want to rescue anyone at all.

---

3 years prior

King Felix rode his horse, Saturn, with a young man bound in chains walking beside him. The prisoner bore a black eye and other marks of a severe beating, evidence of the harsh treatment dealt by the King and his guards.

When they reached the servants' quarters, Felix dismounted, removed the chains, and led the man inside.

From inside the castle, Montgomery and Lilith watched.

Montgomery took a bite of the cow liver the maids had prepared for her lunch. She glanced at Lilith and smirked.

"Quite a looker," she said, pointing her fork toward the newest captive her father had brought in.

Lilith only nodded, offering a distant smile. The conversation made her uneasy; Montgomery's interest was clearly driven by lust.

When Felix returned to the castle, it was clear the fight had not been easy for him either. He sported a black eye and deep scratches across his face.

Upon reaching the women, he spoke briskly.
"Lilith, go check on the boy."

Lilith nodded.

Montgomery dabbed at her chin with the sleeve of her dress. "I shall help the servant, Father," she said quickly.

Felix turned sharply toward his daughter. "I didn't ask you to, Princess. I asked Lilith. And we've discussed this before call her by her name. Why couldn't you be more like your mother!" he roared, before motioning for Lilith to go.

Lilith could tell Montgomery was embarrassed by the scolding, and though Felix had been harsh, Montgomery had never once been kind to her. Lilith found it difficult to feel pity. In truth, she felt a small, guilty satisfaction when Montgomery didn't get her way.

Lilith entered the servant's quarters, where the young man lay in poor condition. She fetched a cool rag from the well and placed it gently on his forehead.

He looked up at her. "Are you an angel?" he asked.

"No, I'm not an angel," Lilith replied with a quiet laugh.

"Well, you're pretty enough to be one," he said quickly.

"Were you taken here too?" he asked.

"Yes. But I don't remember anything before. I've been here my whole life," she answered.

He sighed. "Could you kill me?"

The question shocked her. "I can't kill you," she said at once.

"I don't see any use in living anymore," he murmured. "If I can't even read a book, then there's no point in going on."

Lilith hesitated, then said, "If I brought you a book, would you still feel that way?"

"I suppose it might make life a little less unbearable," he admitted.

"Give me a few days, and I'll see what I can do," she promised. "If Montgomery catches me stealing, I could

be killed, but if it can help you, I will." Her eyes held a steady seriousness.

"I would be eternally grateful," he said.

"What's your name, Angel?" he asked.

"Lilith. And yours?"

"Carac," he said with a faint smile. "After my father."

"It sounds like this guy has been taking advantage of you since he came to the castle. I don't think you should risk your life trying to save him once again," said Luca.

Everything Luca said was true. I agreed, but I still feel like I had to be responsible for Carac. Over the last two years, I made sure Carac did everything for himself. It wasn't for me, the King or Montgomery would have hung him from the gallows. I couldn't imagine how hostile Wilbur would be to Carac without me. Wilbur always thought I was too kind to Carac. He was right, too. Carac didn't deserve a rescue, but I couldn't live with myself if I didn't at least try.

"I know he doesn't deserve it, but I am going to try anyway. I can't just leave him there. I don't want to save him as my lover, I want to save him as one of my only friends," I said, trying to reassure Luca.

Luca sighed. "Well, I don't want you to go alone… and although

I fear you're going to run off into the sunset with him, I'll help you."

I smiled at Luca. "Trust me when I say I will not be running off into any sunsets without you."

This made Luca smile.

I crawled back onto Luca's lap. "Maybe we could talk about what you wanted to talk about earlier," I said as I trail off.

"Hmmmm," he scratches his head and pretends like he forgot.

I kissed him on the lips and waited for his response.

"I always have time to talk about that," He smirked and kissed me back.

"Your beard is rough," I said as I stroked his face.

"I can cut it off," he said quickly.

"Oh. I like it," I said with a smirk.

CHAPTER 22: PLANS

I drew a map in the dirt of the castle courtyard.

"That is where Frog keeps her hordes of food," I said as I drew an X with my stick. Carrot came running up and tried to eat the end of the stick I was using as a tool.

Ebba, deep in thought, didn't seem to notice Carrot gnawing away at my tool and destroying my map. Her brow furrowed with worry at her thoughts.

She finally spoke, "You know the castle grounds better than anyone. I'll trust your best judgment. Are you two sure you all want to do this alone?"

Luca and I nodded.

"I think fewer people will draw less attention to us," I said.

Ebba took us both into her arms for a moment and let us go.

I decided to give Ebba and Luca a moment alone while I readied the horses. I knew Ebba would have a tough time letting her child go.

I grabbed Saturn's reins and Luca's horse and led them out into the grass.

Luca and I were both dressed in black pants and large shirts with long hoods that went past our faces. We looked like shadows coming to life. We stuck out like a sore thumb during the day, but later in the night, when we reached the castle, we would be invisible. The only thing that stood us apart from the night was my flails and Luca's longsword.

When I reached the others, I could tell that Ebba was worried about Luca. She was looking up at him with her hands around his cheeks and telling him something about keeping himself safe.

I took my hand and placed it on her shoulder. "Don't worry, I'll keep him safe," I said with a smile.

She grabbed my hand and squeezed it tightly. "He's my baby, you know," she said.

"I know he is, "I said.

She then hugged me and told me the same things she had told Luca about taking care of himself. It felt nice. I knew I had a mother. It was impossible not to, but I had never had someone like Ebba. I didn't even know what I had missed till I came here.

After we had said our goodbyes, we jumped on our horses, and we were off.

We decided to go through the forest so that many villagers couldn't see us.

―――

Wilbur sat quietly as he watched the horses walk on the forest floor. He could only see their hooves. He tried not to move, but he couldn't help but smile when he heard Lilith's voice.

―――

The sky was beginning to grow dark, so I knew we were close. We tied up the horses to a tree in the forest far away from the castle and sat down on the ground.

"Have you been to the castle before?" I asked Luca.

"No, I have heard many stories about it, but never been here myself., It is beautiful. I wish you could show me around," he said with a melancholy smile.

"How do you think Carac will react when he sees you?" Luca asked.

I thought about it for a moment. "I don't know. I'm not too worried about it, though. I never really meant anything real to him. We were only close because of our circumstances."

———

1 Year Prior

Carac woke up in the middle of the night, and he couldn't fall back asleep. He looked over at Lilith. She was sound asleep. He looked behind his shoulder to make sure Wilbur was still sleeping. Carac moved closer to Lilith and put a piece of hair behind her ear, which made her flutter her eyelids. Carac slowly moved his fingers to his lips in a motion to stay quiet. Lilith smiled back and nodded to say yes.

Carac moved his lips slowly to her ear. "Wanna get outta here?" He whispered.

Lilith nodded and smiled.

They quietly got up and made their way to the gardens.

Carac picked up a purple flower and gave it to Lilith.

"I can't keep this, Frog might find it, "Lilith said.

"That is true, but tonight I want to pretend you can. I want to pretend we are the King and Queen of Utuk," Carac said loudly and unapologetically.

Lilith extended her hand to Carac. "Oh, my beloved, how beautiful the gardens are this time of year," she said in a fancy voice.

Carac, without skipping a beat, placed Lilith's arm around him and pretended to straighten a collar on his shirt.

"My Darling, you look so beautiful in that gown. It must have taken the seamstress a year to make such a garment." He matched her energy.

Lilith pretends to curtsy. "Oh, I don't even know how long it takes to make such a thing. I am the Queen, it doesn't concern me." Then Lilith pretended to pull a fan from her pocket and wave it like the heat of the party was beginning to get to her.

"My queen, if I am to be so bold, I couldn't stop staring at you from across the ballroom tonight." Carac took his finger and ran it across her chest.

"Is that so? Whatever could you be staring at?" Said Lilith as she fluttered her eyelashes.

"Your dress is exquisite, but to be completely daringly honest. Carac moved so close that his lips were touching Lilith's ear. I have been thinking about what you look like out of it," Carac said in his sly voice.

Lilith Blushed, and this time she wasn't pretending.

———

"Circumstances are all it was," I said quickly.

Luca looked at me with his deep brown eyes, listening to every word I said. The only person who had ever listened to me as much as Luca was Wilbur, but it was different when Luca listened to me. I couldn't wait for Luca to meet Wilbur and Detrix; something told me Luca would have a good relationship with Wilbur. Wilbur would be thrilled that I didn't want Carac's company; he would be happy about anyone.

The sun had completely disappeared on the horizon, and the frogs had begun to sing songs of love into the night.

Luca turned to me. "Ready?" He asked. I could tell there was a hint of fear in his voice.

"I'm ready," I replied.

We threw on our hoods and started to creep into the apple orchards from the forest. We crept slowly, not to draw any attention to ourselves. We walked until we were standing in the flower gardens by the castle. I looked over at Luca, and he had a look of childlike wonder on his face. I had been at the castle for so long that I was never fully able to take in how beautiful it truly was.

I leaned over to Luca. "It's pretty, isn't it?" I ask.

"Yes. I have never seen so much color in one place," he said.

"The late queen planted all these flowers..." My voice was cut short.

As I turned to look back up at the castle, I saw him on Montgomery's balcony. Carac.

BACK TO THE CASTLE: PART 10

Carac stood on the balcony outside the castle. He could hear the frogs singing love songs into the night. He took a drink from the bottle of wine he was carrying. He felt a drop of the red wine drip down his cheek, but he didn't care. He was extremely thankful Frog had finally fallen asleep so he could sneak away for a moment. He was so close to the power he had worked so hard for, but the journey wasn't easy. The training with Marquise was taking a toll on him physically and emotionally. It was funny; the only person he wanted to talk to about it was Lilith. He smiled for a moment when he thought about her. Then he returned to reality and took another long drink of the wine. He finished off the bottle and threw it off the balcony, laughing to himself. He looked out into the Kingdom. He thought about what it would be like to be the King. All at his mercy. Then he thought about Montgomery and sleeping beside her for the rest of his days. He climbed up and swung his feet over the edge of the balcony. He looked down, and when he sat back up, he could feel his head swimming from the wine. That's a long way down, he thought to himself. Carac looked down for a second time. I wonder what it feels like. Then he saw her, Lilith, dressed in all black in the gardens. He waved, but she didn't wave back. Then Carac noticed how close he was to the edge and jumped back onto the balcony.

"I hate you, Lilith! I'm here because of you! You're a whore!" He mumbled to himself. Something that wasn't audible. "I'm sorry I am taking you to Marquise. You don't deserve it. I deserve to be here. I deserve to be here. I miss my mother. I miss everyone. I miss you. Please come back. No, don't, Marquise will kill you," He panicked. "Lilith. I want you, but I need power."

Then Lilith ran underneath the balcony. "Carac! Stop talking, you're drunk." He could tell she was sad. She was miserable a lot.

"You're always sad," he said, but he could feel the words slurring.

Lilith looked up at him with tears in her eyes. "Carac, go to bed before you fall off the balcony."

Carac decided that it was a promising idea and returned to

the castle. As he walked through the halls, he touched the paintings and found one of Montgomery. He stared at it for a moment. "FROGGGGGG," he roared.

"You're just a big ol' frog. Look at you." He slurred his words.

He was suddenly overcome with tiredness and lay down on the cool marble floor, falling asleep.

Early the next day, he awoke to Marquise shaking him. "Get up, boy! You got drunk last night, and the Queen is going to notice you're out of bed. You need to keep this lover boy thing up if you know what's good for you. Trust me. We need Frog on our side. Here I made this bread, take it to her. Pretend you got up early to make it." Marquise picked him up.

Carac quickly brushed himself off. As he stood up, he could feel a pain throbbing deep in his head.

"Do you have any idea what I did last night?" He asked Marquise.

Marquise shook his head. "I found a broken wine bottle in the yard and one of the barrels of flour had been open last night, but one of the guardsmen could have done that too," said Marquise.

Carac thought hard about how he had gotten in front of the painting, but he couldn't remember... Lilith? Had he thought about her? Of course, that's why he started drinking in the first place; he was sure he would be thinking about her.

Carac grabbed the bread and briskly walked to Frog's

chambers.

When he opened the large wooden door, he saw Montgomery looking at herself in the mirror. She had not chosen a wig to wear today. He could see her real hair. It was noticeably short and matted close to her head. Carac squinted, and he thought he could see a small bug running through it. He had to push that aside and not think about it.

"My queen, I awoke early to make you this bread," Said Carac.

"Who were you talking to last night?" She asked while she looked directly into his eyes from the mirror.

"I must have been talking in my sleep, dear," He said quickly.

"You said her name... You said Lilith." Said Montgomery

"Hmmmm, I think I know why I was saying her name last night." Said Carac like he was pondering.

Montgomery gave him a stern glare.

"I just remembered I had a dream that I captured the little retch and brought her back here to you," Carac said.

Montgomery smiled.

Carac knew he had sold her on the story, but he wanted to make sure he sunk it in deep.

"After her capture, you took me back up here and we did...

Well, we did that thing we did a few nights ago." Said Carac as he slid himself onto Montgomery's bed,

Frog bought his lie. She climbed onto the bed with him and placed a hand on his face.

"How could I think such awful thoughts about you, puppet?" She said as she brushed her long nails down his cheek.

"Let's celebrate our love with some wine, shall we?" asked Carac.

"Go to the pantry and fetch a bottle puppet," she said.

Carac quickly got up off the bed and went straight to the pantry. This is where Montgomery kept all the food. Carac grabbed a bottle of wine off the shelf and looked at the empty barrel of flour. For his life, he couldn't remember what he had done with that flour last night.

Love

"Is that the prince"? Asked Luca

"Ummm...That's Carac. I have no idea why he is on the balcony. He is extremely drunk."

"Yeah, I think I got that much," Luca replied.

Carac threw the bottle he was drinking from off the balcony and then turned and looked out into the garden, beginning to wave at us.

He yelled out. "I hate you, Lilith! I'm here because of you! You're a whore! Then he mumbled to himself... Something that wasn't audible. "I'm sorry I am taking you to Marquise. You don't deserve it. I deserve to be here. I miss my mother. I miss everyone. I miss you. Please come back. No, don't! Marquise will kill you." He panicked, "Lilith. I want you, but I need power."

Luca looked at me. "That makes no sense," he said quietly.

"I don't think he knows you're here, just stay still for a moment where it's safe," I said to Luca.

I ran underneath the balcony and begged Carac to come down and come with us, but he didn't hear me.

He just kept saying nonsense, so I pleaded with him to at least go inside before he did something awful to himself.

I ran back to Luca, who was sitting in the gardens.

"I don't think I will be able to get Carac to come with us. I don't know what to do. I'm worried Frog will have him hanged if she finds him in the castle drinking her wine," I said to Luca.

Luca put both of his hands on my shoulders. "I don't think that is the same person who was here when you left. He was in a Guards uniform. I don't know if you noticed." Luca said softly.

I shook my head. "He's playing some dress up with Felix's old clothes. I could sneak in and talk him into coming with us."

Luca still had his hands on my shoulders. "Lilith, if you go into that castle, it could risk your life. It is already dangerous enough that we are here. Stealing their food is a risk, but if you go into that castle, we will be caught. You said yourself that the castle itself could be a death trap.

"It's true, but I feel responsible for Carac. Like it's my job to take care of him," I said.

'Why do you feel that way?" Asked Luca

I thought back to why Carac was brought to the castle in the first place, and it made me sick. I didn't have time to explain to Luca.

Luca grasp me, "I must know something. When you kissed him, did it make you feel a surge of heat rise from the soles of your feet to the top of your head? Did you get lost in his eyes when he looked at you? Did you look at him while he was asleep and wonder what he was dreaming?"

"I did all of those things," I said.

"Do you love him now? Because if you love him, I will help you get him," said Luca as he let a single tear slip down. I couldn't tell if the tear was a result of frustration, sadness, or both.

"No," I said.

"How could you have thought all those things about him and not love him now?" Asked Luca

"Because I met someone else. I met someone with whom I fell madly in love. I feel more love for this person than I ever thought I could feel. Not only did I fall in love with them, but for the first time in my life, I fell in love with myself. This person inspires me every day to be a better person than I was the day before. This person motivates me to work hard. This person teaches me how to do things I was told I could never do in my whole life. When I look at this person, I imagine what their face will look like; they are old and seasoned with life, because I hope I am still with them then." I looked at Luca deeply. "This person also keeps me up at night because I can't help but think about being in their hammock with them." Then I winked at him. "I love you, Luca."

"You love me"? He asked.

I nodded.

"I love you, too." He said quietly.

In the moonlight, he leaned down to kiss me. I could taste the salt of our tears on my tongue.

After we had broken apart, I looked back at the balcony one last time to make sure that Carac wasn't coming back. "Let's go get Wilbur." He will be in the slaves' quarters.

When we reached the quarters, there was no one to be found. The little shack that once was home was empty. I dashed to the stables to see if Wilbur was there, but he was gone.

I fell onto my knees in defeat at the stables. I let my tears fall and hit the dusty barn floor. This time, I wasn't crying from joy; I was crying from sorrow and pain. Luca came running behind me.

"Maybe he is in the castle too?" asked Luca.

I shook my head because I couldn't form words from my trembling lips.

"He was never allowed in the castle. I waited too long," I finally managed to get out.

Luca paced back and forth, which made me cry even more because it was what Wilbur did when he was thinking hard in the stables.

It felt like he was there in a way. He was so close I could almost touch him.

Luca picked me up off the ground. "Grieve, Cry, Sleep, Take Vengeance if you will, however. Tonight, we still need to get the flour."

I stopped crying for a moment and got up, wiping the tears from my face. "What was the last thing you said?" I asked Luca.

"Take Vengeance," he said.

"That's what I am going to do," I said quickly.

Luca and I walked to the pantry. I was shaking with a combination of Anger and Grief. I was not paying attention and knocked over a barrel. It made a loud bang on the floor, so Luca and I quickly began filling up our sacks with scoops of flour.

Once we had filled our sacks, we walked as quickly as we could back to the forest. We threw our bags over the horses and started our walk back home.

Luca spoke up. "Is there any chance your friend Wilbur left?"

—

A year prior

Wilbur was sweeping the barn when Lilith walked in.

She walked over, grabbed a brush from the shelf, and began stroking Saturn's long white tail.

"Carac was telling me about his village on the west side of the Kingdom. It sounds amazing," Lilith said.

Wilbur nodded. "It is," he said slowly.

"Do you think we could run away?" Lilith asked Wilbur.

"I think running away would be silly for an old man like me," said Wilbur.

"You're not an old man. I bet you're the same age as the king," Lilith said quickly.

"I have everything I care about here. "I would never want to leave," said Wilbur.

Wilbur stared at the horses for a few seconds and then rubbed between Saturn's ears.

"I would have run away at one time, though. I have my problems with your boy, but when I was a young man, I would have run away." Said Wilbur.

"Why would that make a difference?" I asked.

"I would have gone for love," he said.

CHAPTER 23: CARAC

As we walked through the forest, the sun began to rise, and we mostly stayed quiet, for I had a lot on my mind.

"Now that I know you love me," said Luca smugly.

I rolled my eyes at him. "I might not if you continue with that tone," I said jokingly.

"Why do you feel responsible for Carac? He was a servant or… slave just like you," Luca persisted.

2 years prior

Montgomery was looking at herself in the mirror, brushing her long, dark hair, when she made eye contact with Lilith in the mirror.

"You will <u>not</u> mess this up for me tonight," Montgomery said quickly.

"You're correct, I will stay in the stables away from everyone," Lilith said quickly.

"Then why are you here?" asked Montgomery.

"I am here to help you get on your dress, princess," Lilith added quickly.

She knew Montgomery would need assistance with tying it up at the back.

"Oh, I was just testing you," Frog said quickly.

Tonight, Montgomery would be presented to the world, more specifically, given to the royal Princes, to indicate that her hand would be available for marriage. Lilith found the whole event to be rediculous. She was glad she wouldn't be paraded around in front of a group of men. It was a royal tradition that the princess be the sole unmarried woman at the event. This was the Princess Party, and Montgomery would not be outdone again at her party. Montgomery was tired of her father inviting the servants to the parties.

"Lilith, grab that blue dress from my wardrobe," Montgomery commanded.

Lilith looked at the dress and held it up to her own body. It was beautiful, but it fell far short of fitting the princess.

"My dear princess, I believe the dress has shrunk," Lilith pointed out.

Montgomery looked at the dress in anger. "That is the dress I am to wear," She shouted. Montgomery threw off her undergarments and stood waiting to be dressed.

Lilith did as she was commanded. She helped Montgomery into the dress and pulled the corset so tightly she thought the ribbons would break.

Montgomery knew she should have worn a different dress, because she couldn't sit down from the constraint, but she didn't want to admit defeat.

"Lilith, hand me my wine," Montgomery pointed to the table next to her. Her dress was so tight she could barely move.

She handed the princess her wine and then began to walk to the stables away from the party.

"Where are you going?" Montgomery asked.

"The stables. Where you told me I had to stay." Lilith said sternly.

Montgomery turned away stiffly, trying to be dramatic. Lilith giggled to herself when she had gotten out of earshot.

Lilith picked up a broom from the corner of the barn.

"Oh, of course I would love to dance with you… Broom Prince," she said, and began swaying. She could hear the music drifting in from the party.

Then she looked up and saw a figure standing in the light. She quickly threw her "Broom Prince" down.

It was Felix. He looked very out of place. He was wearing his crown and dressed in a long red robe that dragged on the ground.

"What are you doing?' he chuckled.

"Shouldn't you be at The Princess's Party?" she asked.

He sighed, "I should. How about you come with me?"

"Montgomery would not be happy with me if I came to her party. She has made it clear I am not invited," she said quickly.

"None of those men will want her anyway, and even if they do, it will only be for a merger of their land and ours," Felix quickly said.

He sat down in the dirt.

"You can have my stool, Felix," she said, offering it to him.

"I don't want it, but thank you," he said.

"You don't deserve this life, you deserve to have your party," he said.

The next song began to play.

"Lilith life is too short just to sit and make the princess happy." Said Felix to Lilith, but it was mainly to himself.

Felix felt defeated as he walked through the barn doors and back into the castle. When he walked into the ballroom, he could see all the men huddled in a corner, taking turns drinking wine from the glass chalices. He looked across the room, and the princess was licking icing from her fingers. He just shook his head. A few of the men's fathers also came to the party. They were just as appalled by their children's behavior as Felix was. Felix fixed his collar and approached the men. "Gentlemen, let us not make this night a waste. Let's talk trades."

"Do you all have any servants you would be willing to trade? For goods. Maybe some jewels. I need a young man. A strong one," Felix said, flexing his arms.

"A young man?" asked one King.

"Why in the world would you want a young man?"

They are the absolute worst to tame," said another.

"I need help with the manual labor," Felix said, shrugging.

"I'll trade you a young man for that maiden I saw walking around here before the ball." He said as he fixed his monocle. She looks like she would breathe some life into someone, if you know what I mean, as he winked with his other eye.

Felix raised his hand to strike the man but stopped himself.

"She is not for sale," he said quickly.

All the men could feel the tension in the air.

One man spoke up. "Felix, you were so kind to host this party for our young men. How about I give you a present in return? I have a young man working for me. He has no family or friends. He has no idea who his parents are. He can't read. I think it would be a remarkable thing for him to work for you. His life currently is terrible."

Felix raised an eyebrow. "That would be excellent. Where is he?" asked the king.

"He is currently at my castle, but if you come to pick him up, he is yours. I have enough servants. I found him begging in the streets and felt sorry for him," said the man.

The next day, the King began his journey to pick up his present. He took a few of his guardsmen and Marquise with him.

As they rode, Marquise leaned over and asked, "Why do we need this boy? We have Wilbur the stableman for any extra labor."

The king leaned a little closer to Marquise. "Lilith is growing older, and she is lonely. You should have seen her at Montgomery's ball; she was dancing with a broom by herself. Montgomery doesn't begin to understand what she has. She didn't even try with any of those men yesterday."

Marquise was silent for a moment. "I heard from the guardsmen that after her party, she took the remainder of the wine to their room, and they partied into the night. I am not sure exactly what happened. I am just as disappointed in the Princess as you, Felix."

Felix just shook his head. "What's wrong with her? While she was with the princes, she sat like a frog on a log eating flies."

Marquise laughed, "Felix, you just called your daughter a Frog."

Felix just shook his head and smiled. "I like to think of her as her mother's child. It helps me cope."

When they finally arrived at the other castle, they quickly found the young man they had come for. He had light blue eyes and blonde hair that almost touched his eyes.

He was chained to a post.

Felix jumped off his horse and took the boy's face in his palm.

"What's your name?" He asked.

This surprised the boy, "Carac," he said.

"Give him your water," said Felix to one of the guardsmen.

Carac quickly drank the water as fast as he could. Once he had finished, he looked up at Felix.

"Have you been sent to rescue me?' He asked.

Felix let out a deep laugh."No, I have not. You belong to me and me only, but I have an unusual duty for you."

Carac's heart sank. He tried slung his chains in the direction of the king in anger.

"I want you to be friends with my other servant. I want you to be her companion of sorts." Felix said holding the boys arms down.

Carac looked at the King, puzzled.

"And if you tell her that was your purpose. I will kill you and never think of you again," Felix warned.

"You want me to be a companion with another servant? That's all?" Carac asked.

"Yes," replied Felix.

"Do I have to be honest about where I came from?" Carac asked.

"I don't care if you say you were a prince," the King laughed, finding it a strange request.

Carac smiled. He hated everything he was. He could be anything he wanted to be.

BACK TO THE CASTLE: PART 11

Marquise drew his sword from its sheath and looked at his reflection in the silver. He pulled his lips close to his nose to see if he had any meat in his teeth. He placed the sword back into its sheath and looked at Montgomery to see if she had been paying attention. She was placing rings on each finger on her hand. They were all distinct colors. Marquise couldn't help but notice Montgomery shoving the red ruby ring onto her pinky finger that had once belonged to Felix.

"Did your father give you this ruby?" He asked as he knelt and kissed Montgomery's hand.

"Yes!" She practically shouted.

"Why wouldn't my father give me this?" She said quickly.

"Oh, I was just admiring it," said Marquise. He knew Felix had given it to Lilith.

"I don't know why you would be. It is the smallest of my collection, but it is mine," Montgomery stated.

Marquise pulled a pair of black gloves from his pocket and a carrot from the other. He broke the carrot stick in half and placed the pieces into the pinky fingers of the gloves. He slipped on the gloves, made a fist with both hands, and watched the carrot pieces flop back and forth. Good enough, he thought to himself.

He extended his arm for Montgomery to grasp. He was escorting her to the gathering of royals. Once a year, the royals gather to discuss trading and socializing.

As they walked together down the long, spiraling stairs, Marquise could feel Montgomery shaking.

"This is in your blood, my Queen. Your mother loved the gathering of the royals." Marquise gave a twist to his mustache and smiled, thinking of fond memories in his heart.

Montgomery sighed. "Father never allowed me to do such

things. This is my first one."

Marquise was surprised.

They had now reached the grand ballroom. Several people had already started making their way to the wine and were pouring themselves considerable portions.

One woman, the princess of Alina, bowed before Montgomery. "Dearest Montgomery, I was so dreadfully sad to hear of your father's passing. May he rest in peace," she then raised her right hand to the air as a sign of respect for a fallen warrior.

Montgomery threw a fist in the air loosely and rolled her eyes. The woman, with much confusion and disgust, walked away and began talking to a few of the other Princesses.

Marquise leaned in close to Montgomery, "My Dear Queen. Your...umm. Bold demeanor might be too much for the other royals."

Montgomery tightened her grip on his arm. "This is my castle, and I shall act as I please," she said quickly.

Marquise knew she was frightened, but he didn't know how to help her.

The party went as usual; people drank and talked. Just as the party was about to end, the Princess of Alina approached Montgomery for the second time. "Montgomery, where is your darling brother?" She said with a smile.

"He ran off to play in the woods," said Montgomery.

The Princess gasped and drew her white handkerchief to her lips. 'Why in the heavens is he there?"

"He does what he wants," Montgomery shrugged.

"He's as dumb as the rocks at the bottom of the river, " said Montgomery.

The princess took the back of her hand and slapped Montgomery across the face.

"You, Montgomery, are a disgrace to your Kingdom. How dare you speak about your brother in such a tone? Your brother is like my sister in such ways. She is the kindest soul this earth has ever known," said the Princess.

Montgomery put a hand on her cheek. "You had no right to hit me," said Montgomery.

"Is this why your father hid you away from the rest of us...? Because you have a black heart?" asked the princess.

Montgomery felt her face turn warm with anger. "Leave this party! Everyone must leave immediately," She shouted.

Not a soul in the party besides Marquise heard her. They all continued their conversations and danced to the music. Even the princess had walked away in disgust.

Montgomery went running out of the party in tears with Marquise close behind. Thoughts of her childhood haunted her mind.

12 years ago

An incredibly young Montgomery squashed a butterfly between her fingers.

Felix was sitting in the gardens smoking from a pipe.

He looked over in disgust at his daughter and took a long inhale.

"Look, father! I am squishing them all, I shall make a beautiful butterfly paste!" Montgomery shouted excitedly.

Felix wasn't listening. He looked over and smiled as he watched Lilith slowly pick up the ladybugs and carefully let them crawl across her fingers.

Montgomery looked down at the very dead bugs she had found in the gardens. "I am ready to go inside now, Father!" She said quickly.

Felix finally realized she was speaking. "What is it that you want, Princess?"

"I want to go inside and play with my doll and have lunch," said Montgomery.

"You don't need another lunch," said Felix with a laugh.

"Father, can I go with you to the Banquet tonight?" Montgomery asked and pulled on his pant leg.

Felix's face suddenly grew very harsh. "Princess dear, I have told you this before. You may not. Maybe when you are older," he said coldly.

"But I want to go! The other princesses are going!" She cried.

"Why? Do you want to kill more bugs there? Or do you want to eat the remainder of the dinner? asked Felix.

Montgomery grew red with anger. "One day you won't be able to tell me what I can and can't do!"

"Yes, Princess, when I am dead, you can be the Queen, " Felix said.

The King looked up into the sky and shook his head.

Later that night, Montgomery, in her nightdress, snuck down to the ballroom to get a peek at the party. She saw beautiful girls in dresses and boys in their best royal robes. She looked around the corner and saw the adults drinking and laughing. She could smell the delicious food coming from the room. She opened the door, and she could see a hog with an apple in its mouth.

Just then, Lilith came walking behind her. She was dressed in her best pants and shirt with a flower from the gardens woven in her hair.

"What are you doing here?" Questioned Montgomery.

"I am collecting all the dirty dishes," said Lilith quietly.

"Well, why do you get to go to the party?" Montgomery asked.

"I'm not going to the party, I am just cleaning. I did get to meet a few of the princesses, though! They were genuinely nice," said Lilith with a smile.

Montgomery was outraged that Lilith had been allowed to attend the party. She burst open the door and ran to her father, screaming angrily. Everyone looked up from their drinks and stared for a moment.

The King, obviously embarrassed by her outburst, looked down at her with pursed lips.

One of the King's friends looked down at her with a raised brow. "Is this the Princess?" he asked.

Felix quickly shook his head at Montgomery. Then he promptly turned back to his comrades, "No, she is not my daughter. She is just a servant's daughter. She isn't quite sane, but our servant is so loyal that we decided to keep her daughter around."

Montgomery felt like she had just been shoved down. "But I am the princess!" She shouted.

Felix quickly picked her up, carried her to her bedroom, and dropped her on the bed. "That kind of behavior is why you will never be invited to the royal's party!" Then he locked the door behind himself with a key

Montgomery sat on her bed, crying, listening to the music and everyone's laughter into the night.

CHAPTER 24: CHILD'S PLAY

Detrix sat next to the fire he had built. He was roasting a squirrel that Wilbur had captured.

He smiled and turned to Detrix, "I like it out here. Just us"

Wilbur smiled back, but a hint of sorrow lingered in his eyes. He was happy Detrix was happy, but Detrix was royalty. This shouldn't be heaven for the boy.

Wilbur wondered for a second what Detrix would be like if he hadn't been born the way he was. Would he be ruling right now? Would he have the heart he has now or his sister's? Would he still be the kind soul that he was? Then Wilbur just shook his head, no use in wondering like that. Good thing too, Detrix was the best friend he could think of as a runaway comrade, and although he wished Frog would have treated Detrix better, he was glad Detrix was happy in their little cave.

"Do you want some squirrel, Wilbur?" Detrix asked.

"Oh, don't worry, son, I'll eat the next one I catch," said Wilbur.

"Do you think we should go see if Lilith is hungry?" Detrix asked.

"I am sure she is eating better than we," said Wilbur with a laugh.

I felt like I was moving through sap while everyone around me was moving at the pace of lightning. My grief was weighing me down. We had been back at the fortress for a week, and I had barely spoken to anyone. I hadn't eaten any of the grain we had worked so hard to get.

I was sitting by the creek with my feet in the water when Carrot sat down beside me. She laid her head on my lap. Her little face made me smile. She knew I was sad.

'Hello Carrot," I said.

Her twirly tail wiggled back and forth.

Luca came and sat down behind me, putting his hands on my back. He began tracing circles on my shoulders with his thumbs.

"You want to talk?" Asked Luca

"I know what it's like to lose many fathers at once," said Luca quietly.

I felt a little bit guilty for a moment, out of everyone, Luca would understand what I had been going through. I hadn't spoken more than two words to him since we had gotten back.

"I feel broken," I said.

Luca pulled me into his chest and put his head on my shoulder. Then he reached over to me and put Carrot in my lap.

"It's okay to feel like that sometimes," said Luca.

"I think you would have liked Wilbur," I said as I stroked Carrot's head.

"Tell me about him," said Luca.

"He had a good heart…. Like you," I said.

———

6 months ago

Lilith looked at the silver platter with longing.

Sheets of chestnut brown chocolate had been carefully laid across it and had been sitting in the cellar so it wouldn't melt in the summer heat while the slaves prepared a feast.

"I've heard it's even better than sugary strawberries," Lilith whispered like the chocolate itself could hear her speaking about it.

Montgomery had traded some jewels of her late fathers for it. She had saved it for a special birthday treat for herself and maybe a few people of her choosing; the Queen hadn't yet decided if she would be sharing.

"I don't think she would notice if we had a morsel," Carac reached his arm forward.

"It's not worth it, Carac," Lilith warned.

He put his hands in the pockets of his pants. "You're right," he said begrudgingly.

Detrix ran into the kitchen with his doll in his hand, clutching it below its neck with his fist.

"Can I try the chocolate?" He asked.

"Detrix, you know I don't make such decisions," Lilith said. She was almost aggravated with him for even asking. She knew that he knew he had to ask his sister.

"I don't want to ask my sister. I know she will say no. Like she always does!" Detrix then threw himself into a chair and began pouting.

"Go play outside, Detrix," Carac tried pulling him up from the chair, but Detrix was quite large.

Lilith didn't like it when Carac was mean to Detrix, but at this moment, it would be better for everyone if Detrix got out of the kitchen. "Detrix, you have to be out of the kitchen; you don't want to get in trouble with your sister again."

Detrix begrudgingly got up and left the kitchen.

"Do you want to guard the chocolate or set the dining room?" Ask Lilith to Carac.

"I'll watch the chocolate, I don't think it's going to run away." Carac had a chuckle to himself. He sat down and put his feet on the little table.

"I'm serious!" Lilith urged.

"I know, I know, I won't touch it, I promise!" Carac reassured her.

Lilith hurriedly set up the royal dining room. Hoping the chocolate wouldn't melt at that time, or Carac would be tempted to eat it. He had problems controlling his desires. She poured some wine and lit the long candlesticks they only used for special occasions, and it was finished.

Lilith entered Montgomery's chambers. "The chocolate is ready to be served, my Queen."

Montgomery giggled, something Lilith couldn't recall her ever doing. "I just can't wait. Father always said such things were a waste." Montgomery almost squealed as she spoke.

"Don't serve it until I am seated,' Montgomery commanded.

"Of course, my queen," Lilith bowed.

The queen nearly ran to the table. She almost knocked over the candles. Lilith was able to catch them before they hit the carpet. Montgomery stayed so distracted with her excitement that she didn't even notice.

She sat down in the red velvet chair at the head of the table. "Bring out the chocolate!" She shouted.

Lilith hurriedly walked to the kitchen across the castle. When she walked into the kitchen, the sight that met her eyes made her blood run cold.

Carac was asleep at a small table, and Detrix, with chocolate sheets in both hands, was shoving them into his mouth, which was already full.

"Detrix!" Lilith shouted, awakening Carac.

One tiny square of chocolate was left on the plate.

"I'm sorry," Detrix said, hanging his head.

Wilbur, unaware of the mess he had just walked into, carried a basket of eggs into the kitchen. "I want to look at the chocolate before Frog eats it. I always wondered what this mysterious sweet looks like…" but his words were cut short.

Wilbur set the eggs down. He closed his eyes and let out a long, deep breath. He then grabbed Detrix by the sleeve. "Go wash, admittedly, no playing around, Detrix," Wilbur commanded.

Detrix nodded and left.

"What are we going to do?" Carac asked.

Lilith began crying, "This wouldn't have happened if you hadn't fallen asleep!" Lilith shouted in a rage.

Wilbur quickly picked up the remaining piece of chocolate and began rubbing his hands in it and smearing it around his mouth.

"What are you doing?" Carac seemed almost intrigued by Wilbur's insanity.

Wilbur grabbed the silver platter and walked out to Montgomery.

Lilith grabbed him, realizing what he was about to do. "There's another way," She begged.

Wilbur stopped for a moment, grabbed her hand gently, and removed it from his arm. "There isn't another way, quickly. Carac, go ahead of me and tell Montgomery you found me eating her chocolate.

Wilbur knew Lilith wouldn't.

Carac hesitated for a moment, his gaze drifting to Lilith as if he were questioning in his mind about what to do.

Lilith nodded reluctantly and looked down at the floor.

Montgomery was growing impatient when Carac came bursting into the room, grabbing onto the arm of Wilbur, holding the plate, and Wilbur licking it like a madman.

"Wilbur stole your chocolate!" Carac announced.

Montgomery's face grew red. She stood up and walked over slowly towards the two men.

"On your knees, thief," Montgomery commanded.

Wilbur reluctantly dropped to his knees and placed the platter on the ground.

Montgomery took a whip from her belt and began slashing into Wilbur's back. She slashed him ten times and then commanded him to stand up.

"You will no longer be allowed in the castle. You will only work with the animals." She spat out.

Wilbur bowed his head and went off into the barn to care for his wounds.

Later that evening, Lilith came to lay strips of bandages on his back. Salty tears from her eyes stung Wilbur's wounds, but he didn't tell her.

Wilbur finally broke the silence. "You haven't even asked me what it tasted like," he chuckled a bit, but suddenly stopped because of the pain it caused.

Lilith was confused. "Asked what?"

"What it tasted like." Wilbur smiled.

Lilith was caught off guard again by Wilbur. This time she laughed.

"Well...?" she asked.

"It was delicious!" He said back quickly.

Lilith wiped her tears away. "What did it taste like? Blueberries? Blackberries or a combination?"

"Even better." Replied Wilbur.

———

"Wow. He sounds like a hero," said Luca.

"He was," I say as I take a pebble and throw it into the stream.

CHAPTER 25: HERO

As the pebble hit the water, I could see tiny ripples radiating from the splash and tiny minnows swimming away.

"Poor Detrix...He probably had to watch Wilbur's" …. And then I stopped. I just couldn't bring myself to say execution.

Luca, still listening, took his arms and wrapped them around me.

We were so engulfed in conversation that we didn't notice the older woman walking behind us on an ass.

In a shrill, squeaky voice, we heard "Luca!"

We both turned around.

The old lady shrank her lip in disgust.

"Luca! A tree fell over our home again, "said the woman accusingly.

Luca looked at me and rolled his eyes.

"You know Adula... You should start putting your home far away from all the dead trees, and this would stop happening," said Luca.

I looked at Luca with a question in my eyes.

He wispered to me, "I'll tell you later."

I just shrugged.

"We will be there soon, Adula," said Luca.

"Oh, there is no need for you both to come. The tree isn't that big," Said the woman.

Luca smiled, but I could tell he wasn't happy. "We will both be there soon, Adula, now I'm sure you have things you should be attending to."

The woman angrily flicked the remains to her donkey but

watched us until we were out of sight.

After she was gone, I laughed. "What was that about?" I asked Luca.

"I'm kind of embarrassed to say," he says, taking his hand and rubbing the back of his neck as he smiles nervously.

———

A year prior

Adula appeared around the giant rock that she and her granddaughter were hiding behind. "Okay, Lece, when that knight comes around this boulder, you need to let out a scream in agony. There is nothing more that a man loves than to be a hero to a damsel in distress."

Lece nodded intently, "I should practice, I don't think I should let out an ugly scream."

"Oh, what a good idea, my dear!" agreed Adula.

Just then, the knight came running up on his horse.

Lece and Adula quickly looked at each other.

Lece let out a dramatic moan in agony and then looked at the knight to see if it was believable.

He was so tall. He had curly, dark hair that waved around his face in the wind. His eyes were dark golden brown. He was perfect.

Adula spoke up, "Oh, thank heavens you showed up in the nick of time, dear knight," she said in a worried tone.

"You see, my dear, dear granddaughter was picking apples from this boulder and fell off." She said as she motioned to the top of the rock.

The knight taking in the scene looked up at the tree above them and then back down at Lece.

He stroked his chin. "Well, I think that is an oak tree, so you would have been looking in that tree for quite some time before you found apples."

Adula Panicked, "Well, you see, we have been waiting all afternoon for your help, and in that time, the birds ate all the fruit from the tree."

The knight nodded, and he was at a loss for words.

"What can I do to help you ladies?" He finally mustered up.

Lece took the back of her hand and placed it on her forehead. "Would you be so kind as to carry me back to my village?" she asked.

The knight rolled his eyes and picked her up, throwing her on his horse.

Lece was confused. "Well, I just assumed a strapping knight

would carry me back to my village."

The knight, without looking, patted his horse to start trotting. "No need when I have a horse, " he motioned to the animal.

Adula motioned for her granddaughter to stop talking, "Oh, thank you, sweet Knight. What is your title?"

"Just call me Luca," he said.

Back to the present

"Wow," I said through laughter.

"Yeahhhh" said Luca nervously.

"Well, I didn't know I was in the presence of a heartbreaker," I said.

Luca rolled his eyes.

"Hey! Maybe if you come and help me get the log off their home, they won't come here looking for "help" anymore." Luca said excitedly.

"I think you should go deal with those crazy loons on your own," I said teasingly.

"Come on, you're coming with me," he said, picking me up and carrying me to the stables.

—

"My dear Lece, I think our plans of catching your husband are going south," Adula said,

Lece looked up. She was in the process of dragging a tree into their current home.

Just then, Luca and Lilith came riding up on a black stallion.

Adula "Oh dear Luca, it was so kind of you to come and rescue us."

Luca smiled, "No need to thank me, ladies. My friend Lilith is here to save the day."

Lilith hopped off the horse, picked up the tree, and threw it back into the forest.

Adula and Lace watched in jealousy.
Lilith jumped back onto the horse.

"Good day, ladies," she said as Luca patted the horse, and they took off.

Lecce let out a scream of frustration, "Who is she, and how did she win Luca's affection so early?" Then Lece sat down on the ground in frustration, crossing her arms.

Adula spoke up, "You will win him, darling, just give it time."

"Not now, grandmother." Shouted Lece

"She just needs to go back to where she came from, and where is that stallion from? I know that's not Luca's. That horse looks like it would be used in the royal army." Then Adula and Lece got quiet and locked eyes.

Then, both at the same time, they shouted, "She's the runaway slave!"

BACK TO THE CASTLE: PART 12

M arquise took a long inhale off his pipe, which he was smoking.

"How's Montgomery doing?" Asked Marquise to Carac.

Carac looked at him with a question. "Fine, I guess," Said Carac.

Marquise tapped the tobacco into his pipe. "The King should have been nicer to his daughter, you know," Said Marquise.

"I guess so," Said Carac.

"She also had to live in the same castle with that Monster of a brother," said Marquise.

"Umm.. What's in that pipe you're smoking?" Carac asked.

Marquise knew he had said too much already.

"What's on our agenda today?" asked Carac.

Marquise turned around and looked at the large clock in the corner of the Guards' liar. "We are already getting a late start on our training… I think you should spend the day with Montgomery."

Carac rolled his eyes… "Please teach me something today instead," He begged.

Marquise exhaled a puff of smoke into the air. "You know Montgomery will grow tired of you without proper attention."

Carac nodded. Marquise was correct. He had just been acting strangely the last week or so.

Carac got up from the table and wandered through the castle looking for Montgomery. When he finally found her, she was asleep on the throne. She had one arm propping her head up on her fist and was snoring quietly.

Carac didn't want to wake her, so he lay down on the cool

marble floor and put his hands behind his head. He looked up at the ceiling. He could see beautiful rays of sun peeking through the stained-glass windows.

The combination of the cool marble floor and warmth from the sunlight made Carac close his eyes and fall into a slumber.

He quickly opened his eyes wide, and the room opened even wider than before.

He looked up at Montgomery, but in her place on the throne was Lilith. She was dressed in a purple gown.

"Hello, Carac," she said, smiling.

Carac jumped up quickly but seemed to be going in slow motion.

"What are you doing here?" He asked.

Lilith just smiled and took a drink from a chalice in her hand. "I am the Queen. Why wouldn't I be here?"

Carac thought this was strange, but he didn't want to argue with a good thing. He walked over and took her face in her hands and kissed her.

Once he kissed her, he knew that he was dreaming. "Lilith, darling, I am dreaming. We don't have much time before you're taken from me."

Lilith looked at him, confused. "I'm dreaming," Carac tried to scream, but nothing came out.

When Carac awoke, Montgomery was on top of him with her knees next to his.

Carac let out a yell in fright, which startled Montgomery. He quickly regained his composure.

"Oh, dear Queen, I was having a nightmare. I am so glad I am awake with you," he said as he took a string of Montgomery's wig and started to place it behind her ear, but the hair fell out of the wig and into his hand. Carac quickly tried to wipe away the loose hair on the rug next to him.

Montgomery started kissing Carac's neck and began working her way down his body. Carac looked up at the stained-glass windows and thought about his dream.

James came running through the Guards' liar.

"Hey, who wants to watch Frog and Carac? They are in the throne room again," said James excitedly.

An audible moan could be heard from the entire group.

One of them threw a cup in his direction.

"Get outta here, you freak," shouted another.

James sat down next to Marquise. "Wanna come?" as he pointed to the door.

Marquise looked at him in disgust. "Have you got nothing better to do, boy?" asked Marquise

James looked at him, confused. "Since Felix died, you haven't been any fun. We used to watch the slaves all the time, and now you act better than all of us," said James.

"You're right. I watched the slaves. That was different. Montgomery is royalty," Said Marquise.

James knew he was losing the argument, so when Marquise had grown quiet, he took the opportunity to speak up. He looked down at Marquise's hands. "At least I still have all my fingers," He muttered under his breath.

Marquise slapped him across the face. "That is enough, boy. Now go make us dinner."

―――

Carac, a bit disheveled, picked himself up off the floor.

Montgomery stretched her long arms and yawned.

"How does a walk in the garden sound, M'Lady?" asked Carac.

Montgomery was pleased with his request. She stood up and locked arms with him.

They walked through the gardens and came upon the vegetables.

"Dear Carac, pick me one of those luscious fruits," requested Montgomery.

Carac pointed to the cucumbers. "One of these?" He asked.

"Yes. Pick me the biggest one," said Montgomery.

Carac pulled his knife from his belt, cut the vine from the cucumber, and handed it to Montgomery.

She looked at it in her hand for a moment and then took a massive bite out of the middle of the cucumber.

Carac cringed as if Montgomery had bitten into him.

They looked up and saw two women standing outside the castle.

Montgomery, through bites of her cucumber, motioned for Carac to take care of them.

Carac carefully walked towards them. They didn't get visitors at the castle very often.

They quickly curtseyed as they saw him approach.

Carac smiled. He liked the respect that came with the castle. This is how people should have been treating him his whole life.

The older woman spoke up first, "My dear sir, I am frightened for the people of Utuk's lives."

"And why would that be?" He asked.

Then the younger woman looked up at Carac and batted her eyelashes.

"A slave is running about among all the people. We believe she is living with the knights and pretending she is one." Said the girl.

Carac nodded. Thank you, dear ladies, for coming all this way to share with us. We will address the situation promptly. Would you like some grain for your troubles?" Asked Carac.

They both nodded in excitement.

After he had gotten them a bag of grain, he thought he heard them both let out a giggle as they walked away.

When he walked back to Montgomery, she had finished her cucumber and was licking her fingers.

"I have good news, darling," said Carac with a smile.

CHAPTER 26: LIARS & MANIPULATORS

I swung my flail into a dead tree behind me. I was getting more precise every day. I could hear the blades hitting the soft wood.

"Amazing," Shouted Luca.

He drew his sword and extended it in my direction.

"I challenge you, young maiden, to a duel," said Luca in his deepest voice.

I walked over to my flails and put them back on my belt. "You, my good sir, would be a fool to challenge me to a duel," I roared, but I wasn't as good as Luca at pretending and letting out a laugh.

Luca rolled his eyes. "How am I supposed to practice talking during a fight if you can't be serious for a minute?" He said in a deep voice.

This made me laugh even more.

Luca drew his sword back into his belt. "You know, you can scare a person out of a fight with just your words, " Said Luca

"True," I said.

"I think to talk someone out of a fight, truly, you have to be a liar and manipulator," I said.

Luca looked at me with confusion. "Why do you think that?" He asked.

"Because Felix was," I said.

---

20 years prior

Felix polished his axes with the hem of his shirt and then slid them into his belt.

Marquise looked at Felix from head to toe, "You look like you're ready for a fight," said Marquise.

"I'm ready to look like I'm ready for a fight," Said Felix quickly.

"Felix, we have no hope in this fight. I think surrendering quickly might be our only option. We need to tell your father," said Marquise.

Felix just laughed, "The people of Utuk don't surrender that easily. I can take care of this without my father," said the prince.

"Then please tell me what you are planning on doing," begged Marquise.

"You and I are going to march to the top of the hill and talk to those pirates," Said Felix.

"Talk to fifty men? Just the two of us?" Asked Marquise.

"Yes, now go to the stablemen and get us the two best horses," said Felix.

Marquise came back riding Saturn with a brown stallion trotting behind him.

Felix glared at Marquise. "Get off my horse," he said blankly.

Marquise jumped off Saturn and hung his head.

The men jumped on their respective horses and rode to the top of the hill that overlooked the ocean.

As they approached, they could see the men. They were all large pirates from a faraway land. The men looked harsh from years of being out at sea.

Felix, with complete and utter confidence, jumped off his horse and quickly walked to what seemed like the leader sitting in the middle of the camp.

The man had a patch over his right eye and appeared to be missing some teeth, but his arms were as wide as Felix's legs. His entire body was covered in tattoos. The tattoos were black with designs of stars and skulls. He had three women eating grapes from a vine at his feet. All exotic and beautiful, each in a unique way.

Felix looked up at the man. "Hello," he said.

The man didn't even seem to notice.

Felix drew both axes and flung them towards the man. They landed on either side of the man's head.

Felix now had the entire group's attention. "The King of Utuk sent me," He shouted.

The man didn't seem to be phased. "The King sent his best warrior only for me to slaughter him. What a shame," said the pirate.

He motioned for his men to take Felix.

Felix had to think quickly. "The king of Utuk has a message for you," he shouted.

———

Marquise stood still, watching from a few yards away. He saw Felix hand the giant man a note. The man read the note, and then Marquise watched in amazement as the men quickly packed up their belongings and ran back to the beach, swimming to their ship.

———

Felix looked down at the woman. They were smiling, but one looked him dead in the eye and mouthed "Help," and a tear slipped down her cheek.

"The King also requests a present for the trouble this had caused his people. How about one of these beautiful women?" asked Felix.

"Anything he wants responding" said the pirate quickly.

Felix picked up the girl by the arm and put her on his horse, then began walking back to Marquise.

When they reached Felix, he had many questions.

"What was that? And who is this? What did that note say?"

Asked Marquise

"The King will have my head," exclaimed Marquise.

Felix rolled his eyes. "Well, my father will never find out about our little adventure, and we will save our country. And as far as the note goes. I wrote something to the effect that I was the smallest and dumbest guard in Utuk, and to be expecting one hundred warriors at sunset. Feel free to kill this messenger, he is useless to me," said Felix.

"What if the pirate had called your bluff and killed you? What would I have done, Felix?" Screamed Marquise

Felix didn't even seem to notice Marquise and gave the woman his shirt to cover her body, as most of it was exposed.

Marquise, finally calming down, looked up at Felix. "And what are we going to do with her?" He said, pointing to the girl.

The girl just shivered. Felix brought his hand to his chin and stroked his beard, which was beginning to grow.

"Do you understand me?" Asked Marquise

The girl looked at him scared and nodded her head.

"Maybe Piper would let her stay at his camp for awhile," said Felix.

"You can't be serious...The nomads? again?" asked Marquise.

"Your father has told you on more than one occasion to stay away from the Nomads," said Marquise.

"Good thing he is not here. You are beginning to become a thorn in my side," said Felix sarcastically to Marquise.

Later in the day, after they had reached the nomad camp, Felix greeted Piper with a hug of brotherhood, and they grasped hands.

Marquise felt a surge of jealousy creeping through him. How could Felix be so selfish as to go against his father's wishes? The Nomads were the lowest sect of the Utuk people, and yet, how could Felix love Piper like he did? Why didn't Felix greet him like that at the start of each day? He had spent his whole life training to be Felix's right hand, and Felix didn't even care.

CHAPTER 27: HEAVEN

I picked a berry and put it in the basket between Luca and I. "Have you thought anymore about the battle?" I asked.

"I know we're almost out of grain again," said Luca.

I nodded.

"We can't sneak in and out of the castle forever. We will eventually get caught," I replied.

"You're right. We are only doing good for ourselves anyway. The people are starving. If we are only getting grain and seed for ourselves, are we any better than Montgomery?" he asked slowly.

I hadn't even thought of it that way, which made me feel a little guilty.

"Even more reason to go," I said.

"What's the plan?" Luca asked.

"Storm the castle and take everything, and prison Montgomery seems too simple, doesn't it?" I said with a laugh.

"That's something of a story book," said Luca with a smile as he popped a berry into his mouth.

"I think we should go in disguise," I said.

"I think we should ride in our best horses fully dressed in weapons drawn," said Luca with a little bit of childlike enthusiasm.

The thought made chills rush down my spine. The thought of all the Knights running over the hillside seemed incredible. I could see myself flail shining in the light, leading the guards up to the front of the castle. Horses would be running so fast that it would seem like thunder had come all the way down to the earth.

"You like this idea, don't you?" asked Luca

"Well, I do. But I also can imagine the guards running out at Montgomery's command and killing us on the spot," I said.

"What if we did both?" Said Luca

"You mean half the guards sneak in and the other half ride in on horseback?" I asked.

"Exactly," he says.

"I don't know. I feel like a bigger group is scarier than a smaller group," I mumbled.

Luca sat down on the cool grass out of the sun. "Come sit with me," he said.

"It's on your head when we go back to your mother's with no berries, then," I say loudly enough so they all can hear me.

"Now, why did you have to go and say that?" He said, pretending to be mad at me.

"I think they like me more than you," I said as I sat down.

"Umm... I know they do. Because you do everything they ask," he said as he put his arms behind his head.

"What if we all die?" Asked Luca

It was thought we were both having but hadn't said yet.

"It's better than dying of starvation and watching everyone around us doing the same," I said.

He leaned over and kissed my forehead.

"When do you think we should go?" Asked Luca

"Well, the others have been ready for 2 weeks. I think they have been waiting on us." I said.

"How will they want this fight to go?" I asked Luca quietly.

"They will want to give the castle a chance to surrender first," he said.

"Ebba will want to go alone," he said, and then trailed off.

I quickly interrupted him, "We both know that's a terrible idea," I said.

"I know, but it's just how she is. She thinks everyone should have the option to surrender, even if they have been ruthless," he said.

I nodded.

"I say we took one last night to ourselves. To live in this little heaven, we have created with each other. And then plan our battle out tomorrow and strike the next night." He said.

"I think that sounds like a wonderful plan, Luca," I said as I twirled his curly hair around my fingers.

"Oh… and one rule," he said quickly.

I raised my eyebrow, "Since when do you give me rules?" I asked with a small laugh.

"No talking about this tonight. You know. Starvation. Battles to the death or anything like it," he said, making remarkably close eye contact with me.

"Okay, fine. I think I can stick to this rule," I said.

"Well, I need time to get ready, " He said as he jumped up.

"Get ready?" I asked.

"Yes. This might be my last date for a while," he says matter-of-factly.

"I tried not to think about how true this statement was. "Well, I guess I need to get ready for the night too," I said.

I walked to the fortress, where I found my hammock and satchel, filled with the things I had collected since arriving at the Knights. My two favorite things are the purple shirt and pants made by the Nomads and the necklace given to me by Luca. I decided to wear them both tonight.

I grabbed a bar of soap from my bed and went to the river to freshen up before our night.

When I turned around, there was Carrot, wagging her little tail. I petted her head. I had come to love this little creature so much. I couldn't imagine not having her in my life. I thought about everything and everyone I had come to love since being here.

I bathed in the river and washed all the juices from the day of berry picking. The cool water felt amazing on my hot skin. Once I was done, I got out and put on my purple silk pants and shirt. I couldn't believe how beautiful it was. It looked like it had been made for a queen. Well, not a Queen like Montgomery, but a good queen.

I looked up and saw Luca; he was on Saturn and extremely handsome. He was in a white shirt that flowed into the sleeves. The garment was very striking against his dark skin. He was wearing black pants that were tight on his thighs. I had never seen him wearing this outfit.

I walked up to him and extended my hand. He pulled me onto the stallion in front of him like it was nothing.

We started riding, and I felt my hand shaking a little. I was nervous, but I didn't have any reason to be.

As we rode, Luca took one hand off the reins of the stallion and gently grabbed my hair and moved it to the front of my body, so my neck was exposed to him.

He moved his lips close to my neck and then whispered, "Where do you want to go?" He asked.

"I would go anywhere with you, Luca," I whispered back.

"I know just the place," he said.

As we rode, I could feel the crisp night beginning to set in.

We approached a meadow and could see fireflies beginning to light up the sky.

"This is beautiful," I said in amazement.

"Not as beautiful as you," he said.

I rolled my eyes because I couldn't help but feel he might be trying to sweeten me with his words, but I didn't want to tell him to stop.

He jumped off Saturn and helped me down. Luca reached into his saddlebag and pulled out a blanket and a bottle of wine.

"I don't think I have seen a real wine bottle since I was at the castle. Where did you get that?" I asked.

"A true Knight never gets up his secrets." He said as he poured the wine into the two glasses he had brought.

I took his blanket and laid it down overlooking the meadow.

I sit down, and he brings the cups of wine over to me. He hands me one.

"For you, the most beautiful woman in all of Utuk," he said.

I smiled and took a sip. The wine tasted amazing.

"Lilith, before the wine takes hold of my tongue, I have to tell you something," Luca said in a serious tone.

"Tell me," I almost begged.

You've filled my life with a meaning I never knew I was missing. I can't imagine a single day without you you're the first thought that greets me in the morning and the last that lingers before sleep. Before you, my daydreams were only of myself, of my own path. Now, every dream, every hope, is colored by you. I see us, together, in every tomorrow. I am hopelessly, wrecklessly in love with you," Luca professed.

Emotions overtook me. At that moment, no land needed saving. There was no Montgomery. There was nothing but Luca. I put my hand on his bare chest where the fabric of his blouse was beginning to meet his skin. He placed a hand on my waist. It was only my waist, but my senses heightened with even the slightest touch from him. His hand felt warm, as if it might burn through my clothing; there was such heat in his palms.

I reached my hand to his jaw and pulled him into a kiss. His lips gently touched mine. He tasted like warm nectar.

Luca gently pulled away and put his hand in his lap.

"What's wrong?" I asked.

He turned and looked me. "I can feel your essence."

"Do I have a bad essence? Are you not attracted to me, Luca?" I asked confused.

"Oh no. It's not that at all. It's quite the opposite. I want you, Lilith. I want you so bad it hurts me. I can feel the heat from your body and the smell of a woman in longing. I don't want to do something you aren't completely sure you don't want to do," He confessed.

I sat down with my wine, which was a simple drink. "I want you, Luca," I exclaimed quietly.

He chuckled at my exclamation. "Are you sure?" He asked again.

I was now growing frustrated with his questions, but I took a breath of air and grabbed Luca's hand, pulling it to my chest.

He looked me in the eyes, his expression a mix of fear and anticipation, as if he were about to devour a meal.

He closed his eyes, as if the air were engulfing him. He carefully took his other hand to my back and laid me down. I felt fragile, like a porcelain doll, but safely protected, like Fine China dishes. We began kissing again, and a moan escaped my lips as he started kissing my neck and his hands worked their way into my blouse. He began unlacing my shirt from the front as he put his body over mine. He looked down at me, staring in awe for a moment, and then took a breath, as if he couldn't decide what to do next. I was pinned to the ground, I looked at his shirt, and he knew I wanted to feel his body on mine. He threw his shirt to the side and pressed his chest against mine kissing me again. My arms were wrapped around his back.

Then I saw Carac standing above him like a ghost. I blinked twice trying to make it go away.

Then, like a flash of lightning, the world went blank.

BACK AT THE CASTLE: PART 13

Montgomery paced back and forth in the castle hallways. She could feel a sweat beginning to form on her forehead. She wanted to know that Lilith was in her hands and gone from her sight forever. If she slipped away from Marquise and Carac, she didn't know what she would do. She had trouble sleeping at night when she thought about Lilith running througyhout the Kingdom. Her Kingdom.

Then she thought back to how strong Carac had grown since his training with Marquise. And Marquise was the most intelligent man she had ever known. How could that brat get away?

Montgomery had always hated Lilith. She had always had what Montgomery couldn't.

---

15 years prior

"Montgomery, dear, go fetch your father his pipe," said Felix.

She threw down her dolls. "I am busy right now, Father," Shouted Montgomery

Felix sighed and began to get off his throne, but before he could get up, Lilith had already brought it to him.

He smiled down at him, "Oh, thank you, child." He put his hand on the top of her head and messed up her hair.

Lilith handed Felix a leaf she had picked from the trees growing outside the castle.

Montgomery watched as her father carefully took the leaf in his large hands. He studied it for a moment and then placed it in a large book by his throne.

Montgomery huffed loudly to get the attention of her father, but he didn't seem to notice.

"Look, father! Look what my Dollie can do," She shouted.

Montgomery had an idea. She ran all the way out into the garden and found the most enormous rock she could carry and began rolling it up the hill to the castle.

She carried it up the steps to the throne room where her father was sitting and placed it at his feet.

"For you father," said Montgomery.

Felix looked down at her. "Why did you bring this disgusting, dirty rock into my castle?" He asked.

"It's a present for you," she said, motioning to the rock.

"Princess, please don't take large rocks into the castle," said the King.

He laid his pipe on the arm of his chair. He picked up the rock and threw it off the balcony.

"How about you play with your dolls, Princess?" asked Felix.

Montgomery hung her head.

———

When I awoke, both my hands were tied behind my back tightly with chains. My mouth was gagged, and I was thrown over a mule.

I started squirming, trying to free myself. I didn't know where

I was. The last thing I remembered was that I was with Luca in the meadow.

In great strength, I pulled my head up and saw. Carac? And Marquise?

As soon as I saw Marquise, I began trying to throw myself off the mule. Even if I were trampled to death, it would be better than wherever Marquise was taking me.

I could see his nasty squirrel-like moustache.

Carac turned around and looked at me when he saw me struggling.

"Lilith, please stop," he begged.

I tried to yell, but it was so muffled it barely made any sound.

I could see the castle in the distance, and a surge of dread filled my chest. I looked for Luca to see if they had captured him too, but I didn't see him.

"Don't worry, Doll, we didn't take your pretty boy with us," Said Carac as if he knew what I was thinking.

I looked at Carac.... He looked different. He looked rough, like his soul was gone. Maybe it had always been gone, and I was just seeintg him for what he was.

I wondered if they had killed Wilbur. They had never gotten along very well.

As we approached the castle, my heart began pumping fast.

We reached the gardens. There was Frog in all her glory.

She must have dressed up for the occasion. She was wearing her white ball gown. James was carrying an umbrella over her head.

Marquise pulled me off the mule and placed me at her feet.

She looked down at me and smiled, but it looked more like a snarl. "Thought you could escape, could you, Lilith?" she said with a condescending tone.

I stared directly into her black eyes with the most mincing look I could muster.

"Don't look at me, slave," She screamed.

I just kept staring.

Montgomery looked at me closely and walked around me.

"Where did you get these clothes?" Slaves aren't supposed to have silks.

"I never had a garment this extravagant. I want it," She exclaimed.

"Take her gag out, darling, so I can see where she stole it from," said Frog.

I was curious to see who her Darling was. She had said it in such a tone that whichever one it was, she thought it would upset me.

Carac hesitated and then came forward and untied it.

"Darling?" I whispered as he bent down.

"I didn't have a choice," he said quickly and quietly.

Marquise caught him commenting and glared at him.

Why does he care about Frog, I thought to myself.

"Where did you get this from?" Shouted Montgomery for the second time.

"They don't make these to fit swine," I finally said.

"How dare you?" Screamed Frog.

I knew she would order one of the minions to put my gag back on, so I decided to cut her deep in case I never got the chance again…

"It doesn't matter how bad you treat me, Montgomery, it will never make your father love you," I said as I gritted my teeth.

Marquise jumped up. "Montgomery, you know that isn't true," I heard him shout.

LILY BOONE

Then he swung his fist into my temple, and I was out again.

CHAPTER 28: THE SWORD

When Luca awoke, he could feel pain on one side of his head. He looked up and saw that he was sitting underneath a tree. He didn't recognize the place he was, which sent panic down his spine. Luca quickly tried to get up, but realized his hands were tied behind his back. The more he struggled to free himself, the tighter the constraints became.

"What was the last thing he remembered? He thought hard. Lilith. Oh my. Lilith. Had the monsters that took him tied her up as well?" His thoughts raced.

He felt such agony in his heart. "What have they done with her?" He thought.

"How could he have been so selfish?"

He felt no better than an animal. This was his fault he thought to himself; someone had taken her. He was supposed to be protecting her. He was a knight. She had chosen him to love. How could he just let someone sneak up and take her from his arms? He began to let tears of frustration run down his face. He decided he was going to rescue her, even if it meant spending his last breath doing it. He hoped that she could find it in her heart somewhere to forgive him for letting her slip away.

"Lilith!" He shouted, but he felt his voice crack. His voice was weak as if he had been running a long distance.

He felt utterly helpless but didn't stop yelling.

Detrix poked Wilbur. "He's up! What should we do?" he asked in a whisper.

Wilbur stretched his arms wide. "Well, he sure is hollering, isn't he?" He replied.

"Here, put this gag over his mouth, so we don't have to listen to him," Wilbur mumbled.

Detrix put the gag over his mouth. Luca struggled against it, but he wasn't much of a fight with his hands tied behind his back.

"Why do we have to keep tied up?" Asked Detrix

"Well, he was asleep in a meadow when we found him. He had a bottle of wine that looked like it was from the castle. I think that's what he traded Lilith for. I bet he was celebrating his victory. The dirty scoundrel," Scoffed Wilbur.

"Maybe that's not what happened," Said Detrix

"Trust me, no man goes out into a meadow by himself with a bottle of fine wine unless he was celebrating something," said Wilbur.

"He was saying something about Lilith when I put the gag on his mouth," Said Detrix

"Good, I'll start asking him who he sold her to, and we will be one step closer to rescuing her...What good is a man that steals another man's horse?" Said Wilbur as he stroked Saturn's mane.

Saturn nuzzled back into his hand.

"Hey! he's got sword on his belt and a satchel on his side," Shouted Detrix

"Well, see what's in there," Wilbur shouted back.

Detrix pulled out some bread and threw it to Wilbur from the satchel.

"Lunch is on the scoundrel today," Shouted Wilbur to Detrix.

"Come look at his sword! It's shiny!" shouted Detrix.

Wilbur walked over, looked down at Luca, and pulled out the sword. He quickly dropped the bread with his other hand.

Luca squirmed around trying to deter Wilbur from taking his sword. His eyes were blood shot.

"Don't drop our lunch," Detrix shouted.

Wilbur didn't hear him. There wasn't a person alive that Wilbur could have heard at that moment.

"This is my sword," said Wilbur quietly as he ran his fingers along the swords handle.

———

25 years prior

"Wilburn, the time has come for you to construct your sword," Mark Head of the Knights of Basil announced.

Wilburn looked at him. In pure glee. "Are you sure, teacher?" He asked as he bowed his head.

"I am always right," The man said with a smile.

"You will need to go to the blacksmith and learn the trade and come back when your sword is complete," said the man.

Wilburn of Basil nodded.

"When you see me again, I will have constructed the best sword the world has ever seen.

—

Wilbur took the sword out of its sheath and looked at the handle. He drew his finger lightly across the blade and watched as a drop of blood hit the ground.

"Oh, love, you haven't lost anything," he said, as if the sword itself would respond.

Detrix had begun eating the bread Wilbur had dropped and was staring at him.

Wilbur finally seemed to snap out of his trance, but his hands were still shaking.

He put the sword into his belt and smiled.

Then he remembered their prisoner, and his face grew red with anger.

Luca looked up at the two men in front of him. The larger one had put a gag on his face and then walked away. It was very strange.

He heard them whispering about rescuing Lilith, which was

quite confusing.

"How did these men know Lilith?" he thought to himself.

They wanted to rescue her from their conversations, so whoever took her was someone different.

Then he thought hard about who Lilith had told him about. "Could it be?" He thought to himself.

"Could this be Wilbur and Detrix? It must be! Oh, he must have them!" He gleefully thought, But the gag was over his mouth. "How was he going to tell them?"

Then Wilbur came running to him and ripped the gag from his mouth.

"Where did you get this sword?" Wilbur demanded.

"That's mine. Get your hands off it," shouted Luca, after feeling the heat from Wilbur he quickly pushed away the thought that this man might be the honorable Wilbur Lilith had spoken so highly of.

Wilbur let out a chuckle. "This is mine, boy. Now tell me. I must know where you found it".

"You can't get another sword like it. Don't bother asking," said Luca.

"I know you can't get another one like it, you scoundrel! Because I spent a year of my life constructing this sword. I melted the metal with my hands. I forged the handle. I must know who you got this from," shouted Wilbur.

"You're a filthy lying man," shouted Luca. His eyes grew with hate and spit was flying from his mouth when he spoke.

"My father made that sword. It was the only thing I have from him, and I'll be damned if I let you take it from me," Shouted Luca. Luca nearly freeing himself from the ties in a rage.

Wilbur looked at him deeply for the first time in confusion.

He quickly untied Luca.

Luca, confused, looked at his freed hands and then back at the man standing before him. Luca was now standing still.

Wilbur looked at the boy's eyes, and he had seen those eyes before. His beautiful bride, so many years ago. He looked at the boy's hands. They were rounded and firm like his own.

Wilbur began to cry, "You've got your mother's eyes," he said.

Luca grasp Wilbur shoulders and then Luca began to cry because he knew. This time from a happiness and realizing he had been missing a large piece of himself for a very long time. This was his father, and he had to be Wilbur.

The two men embraced as if to make up for the lifetime they had been apart.

"Oh, I can't wait to tell Lilith," shouted Luca with glee.

"I'm in love with Lilith," Luca said excitedly.

Wilbur's heart was overflowing. He was at a loss for words to express himself.

The men broke apart for a moment… "We are going to get her back…together," said Wilbur.

CHAPTER 29: REUNITED

Detrix was puzzled to say the least when he saw Wilbur and the Prisoner walking with their arms on each other's shoulders.

The Prisoner quickly sat down next to him.

"You must be Detrix!" he shouted excitedly.

Detrix looked at him with a question, then at Wilbur as if he were asking if he was safe. Wilbur nodded.

Detrix carefully took the prisoner's hand and shook it lightly.

"I am Luca. Lilith had told me so much about you," Said the man.

"Really?" Detrix was so excited to hear what Lilith had said about him.

"She says you're the greatest Prince Utuk has ever seen," said Luca with a smile.

"Well, not very many people think that" said Detrix, and then hung his head.

"Do you know where she is?" Detrix asked in a hopeful voice.

Luca's eyes grew sad. "I don't, but together I know we can," Said Luca

Luca patted Detrix on the shoulder and then picked himself off the ground to speak to Wilbur.

"The knights of Utuk are planning an attack on the castle very soon," Said Luca

This got Wilbur's attention. "When?" he asked.

"I'm not sure, but with Lilith and me disappearing, I'm sure sooner than later," Said Luca.

"They will be quickly killed if they go in front of the castle," exclaimed Wilbur.

"That's what Lilith said... We must tell them now," Luca sighed.

Lead the way," Wilbur motioned for them to go down the road.

"Did I tell you I'm also a knight?" Asked Luca

Wilbur smiled. I already knew.

Wilbur's face grew solemn for a moment.

"Is Kato with the knights?" he asked.

"Who is Kato?" Asked Luca

———

Luca's Birthday

Kato awoke in the middle of the night and looked at her husband, Wilbur..

He was already awake and appeared to be listening to the sounds of the night.

Wilbur, realizing she was awake, quickly walked to her and knelt beside the bed, grabbing her hand.

"Did I wake you?" He whispered.

"No… The baby did," She said as she took the covers off the bed and put her legs to the side.

Wilbur took his hand to her stomach and felt the baby moving inside.

"She's moving," He said.

Kota smiled back at him. "HE is a boy, we have already talked about this before."

"How do you KNOW it's going to be a boy?" asked Wilbur

"I just know…" She said.

Wilbur smiled and kissed Kota on her forehead. "I believe you."

Just then, Kota felt a surge of pain and took a quick inhale.

Wilbur's eyes opened wide.. "Is it time?" He asked.

Kota's eyes swelled. "Yes. It's time," She said excitedly.

Wilbur gave her one last kiss and ran out to find the midwife in the village, but that's when he heard pain coming from shelters next to him..

A man drenched in blood went screaming and running through the village. He had a baby tied to his back, which made the scene even more confusing. The infant was screaming in terror.

It was then that Wilbur's comrade and fellow knight ran up to him and pointed to the hillside. What Wilbur saw sent a shiver down his spine. It was covered by about thirty men running towards them. The men were armed with knives and torches.

They had no chance against these men. There were only fifteen people in their small village.

Wilbur had to think quickly. He didn't know he could survive this, but Kota could.

He ran back to Kota and picked up his sword along the way.

"What's going on?" Asked Kota

Wilbur didn't have the time to answer her, so he picked her up and ran out to his best horse.

It was then that Kota saw the men running across the hillside.

Wilbur quickly helped her on the horse and handed her his sword.

"You must ride away from here," He said through his tears.

"I won't go without you," she said.

"Go for him," and Wilbur placed a hand on her stomach.

Kota grasped Wilbur's hand for the last time. "I love you," she shouted.

Wilbur squeezed her hand back, then let go and smacked his horse so that it would run. "I love you, Kota," He screamed back.

"Kota is your mother," said Wilbur with sorrow in his voice.

Luca nodded and looked down at the ground. "I never knew her," He said.

"Just the stories the knights have told me," said Luca.

"What did they say?" asked Wilbur.

Luca thought for a moment and swallowed..

"They told me they answered the door in the middle of the night, and a woman was standing there holding me and appeared to have just given birth. She handed me over to them, and then she handed over the sword she was carrying. She said I was the son of a brave warrior, and the sword was mine. They tried to carry her inside, but she collapsed right after... and didn't wake... Our doctor tried everything..." Said Luca as he trailed off.

Wilbur nodded.

"I'm so sorry," said Luca.

Wilbur shook his head. "Oh boy, there is nothing you should

be sorry for. I wish she were standing here with you instead of me."

"They didn't know where she was from or her culture, so they gave her a warrior's burial service," Luca said trying to comfort Wilbur in any way he could.

Wilbur nodded in approval… "She knew you were going to be a boy by the way," He said with a smile.

BACK TO THE CASTLE: PART 14

I felt like I was living my own personal nightmare as Carac walked me to the kitchen. My hands were tied behind me with heavy chains. When we reached the kitchen, I stood and waited for Carac to chain me to the post in the center of the room. This was also the first time we had been alone since before I left.

"I guess a lot has happened here," I mumbled.

"Why did you leave me?" He whispered.

"I didn't leave you, Carac, Frog was going to give me to the guards.. I didn't have a choice," I said quickly.

Carac just shook his head. "I thought I meant something to you."

"Why do you care? You have Montgomery, now," I stated. The whole situation was almost funny. I knew he despised the queen.

Carac took his hand through his blonde hair. "You know that wasn't my first choice," He said with agitation in his voice.

I could tell he was embarrassed, but he also had the upper hand. I was chained to a post while he walked free through the castle.

"Do you think she loves you? Are you really that naive?" I asked.

"I don't think she will ever be capable of loving anyone besides herself." He said as he wrapped the chain around the post.

He stopped once the chain was tight and sat down just far enough that I couldn't reach him.

"Do you love him?" He asked, but I could tell he didn't want my answer.

I just stared at him in silence.

"Fine, don't tell me then," He said as he walked away.

Then he turned around.

"Did you ever love me?' He asked quietly.

"Did you love me?" I asked.

"I asked first, " he said.

"You know it's funny, He asked me if I loved you," I said.

"So, you told him about me?' Asked Carac

"I guess I did. How couldn't I? We only had each other, you, me, and Wilbur." I felt my voice tremble.

"That answers my question," Said Carac

"How does that answer your question?" I asked.

He sighed. "You told him about me because you love him, and you wouldn't have told him about me unless you loved me. You felt like you owed him."

"I don't know, Carac, maybe you're thinking too deeply on this." I sighed.

"Did you tell Montgomery about us?" I asked.

"No, I didn't. But how couldn't she know?" He said quickly.

"Why didn't you just tell her?" I asked.

"Because I don't love her," he said in a frustrated tone.

I looked down at the tiles on the floor. "Carac, I didn't do anything to you, I didn't take you here, I didn't ask Felix to take you here… You know that."

Carac started pacing the floor and then stopped in front of my feet. Then he asked again, "Why didn't you take me with you. You could have snuck in and gotten me out."

I thought about it for a moment.

"I knew Montgomery would be angry if you came with me, so I didn't ask," I said.

"I did try to help you one night, and you were drunk on the balcony and didn't want to come with me. I screamed Why don't you run away now?" Go back to your family. Montgomery lets you run free now." I said.

"I lied," He said.

"I never had a family. They sold me when I was a baby to buy food for their older children. I would have nowhere to go," said Carac.

I nodded. "You know, they thought you would live a lavish life in the castle serving a King."

He cut me off, "No, they left me. Just like you left me here," He thundered.

"Montgomery is never going to leave me. Once she has done what she wants with you, we are going to get married, and I shall be king over this land."

Carac's tone scared me. His tone had changed. His thirst for power had overtaken any emotions he had left.

I felt pity for Carac. He was never really going to have what he needed. He needed someone to love him.

Then Montgomery yelled for him, and he left the room.

I leaned on the post, looked over towards the hall, and saw Marquise watching me from the hall.

"What do you want?" I asked loudly in his direction.

"You have a cunning eye, Lilith," Said Marquise as he pranced slowly into the room.

"How long have you been there?" I asked him without looking up.

"Long enough to hear your and Carac's conversations," he said, taking his thumb and forefinger to run them along his upper lip.

"Did you find them incredibly shocking or fascinating because you're continuing to stand there?" I asked.

Marquise laughed like he was clever. "I have never found

anything about you fascinating," he said.

"You will no longer speak to Carac.. The queen is finally having some joy in her life without you.. Or Felix... You should have been more thankful to her as a child," He said.

"Carac is a slave just like me. I don't even know why Montgomery would want him. She could have a Prince of her own, for that matter," I exclaimed.

"We both know why she wants Carac," said Marquise.

"I do?" I asked.

"Because he belonged to you.. Everyone here knew Felix brought him for you and you only," Said Marquise.

"When he went on his travels, he never even once brought anything back for Montgomery," Said Marquise

"Montgomery never wanted anything to do with her Father. She would have eaten anything he brought back anyway!" I yelled out. I couldn't help but let out a small chuckle to myself.

"How dare you speak to me like that. She wouldn't have been that way if Felix loved her," said Marquise in a condescending tone, which was driving me up the wall.

"What are you going to do? Chain me up until you decide on how you want to kill me. I know how the castle works. I know my days are numbered. I don't have anything to lose." I said quickly.

Montgomery and Marquise were both so arrogant that I couldn't stand it. Why did Marquise care so much about the Queen? He was just a king's guardsman. Felix was dead. I didn't even know why he was still there.

MARQUISE: PART 1

Marquise watched as Prince Felix cut his steak with his knife and then brought the morsel to his lips.

"Gracious Marquise, why have you always got to be watching me?" Exclaimed Felix

"I just like to keep you safe," said Marquise.

"Well, I'm safe here inside the castle," Said the Prince as he sighed.

The King slowly walked into the room with his long robe

dragging behind him. "Felix, the time has come for you to collect your bride."

Felix shoved his plate across the long table in anger, "I don't want to marry Cousin Matilda."

"Felix, we have talked about this.. This topic is not up for discussion. You already married Meredith when you were just a small lad. The time has come to consummate your marriage," replied the king.

"I don't even remember what she looks like..." mumbled Felix.

"Let me find a bride in the Kingdom," Felix said quickly.

"My son will not be marrying a commoner," scoffed the King.

"You will go tomorrow, take a white horse, so Meredith will know it's her beloved." Then the King turned and walked out of the room.

Felix threw his fists on the table and yelled out in frustration.

Marquise didn't know what to say. He calmly grasped his fingers together and looked up at Felix.. When he saw Felix angry, it sent a rush down his spine.

"I need some time alone, Marquise," Felix said, laying his head down on the long table.

Marquise didn't understand why Felix could hate his life so badly. He would give anything to be him for just a day. Then he had an idea.

"Felix.. Would you like me to get Meredith for you? I won't tell the King, I promise," Marquise asked in a timid voice.

The Prince pushed his forehead off the table and looked at Marquise.

"That sounds like a wonderful idea.. But I don't think it will work," Said Felix.

"I'll let them know you have fallen a tad ill and couldn't make it," Said Marquise

"You can't tell my father," Felix said quickly.

Marquise ran to the chair beside the Prince and put his hand over Felix's fingers. "Trust me. I won't let you down."

Felix looked down at his hand and raised his eyebrows. Marquise looked down at their hands and then quickly crossed his arms.

"Okay, Marquise, I trust you. Tell them I have fallen a tad ill, but I wanted to be prepared for consummation day. I think that Cousin Meredith will believe that. I have a few social affairs I need to attend to before this marriage is final," Felix said.

Marquise nodded. "Where will you be?"

Felix rolled his eyes. "You know where I'll be."

Marquise felt a little sick to his stomach thinking of Felix with the nomads without him. "Let's get this going while the day is still young," he said, swallowing.

Marquise and Felix went out into the stables and rode off together over the hillside until they were out of sight, then parted ways. Marquise watched as Felix rode off into the distance and sighed. He looked down at the gorgeous white mare he was riding. This was the Prince's horse. He had never ridden her before. Then an idea struck him. Marquise laughed quickly to himself because he couldn't control his glee.

Marquise rode for 2 days, stopping only for water and rest. He reached the castle of Meredith's family. He took a deep breath and jumped off his horse. He tied her to a post and then fixed his collar.

He walked up to the large gates to the castle, and as he took each step closer to the door, his chest began to beat faster.

When he finally reached the entrance, he took the large door knocker in his hand and loudly banged three times.

The door opened. The girl who greeted him, he could only assume, was Princess Matilda. She had brown, pin-straight hair. Her eyes were a deep, rich green, and her skin was fair like the snow. Her waist widened at the bottom and curved. She looked different than any other Princess Marquise had ever seen, and for a moment, he completely forgot what he was doing. He shook his head and then quickly introduced himself. She was wearing a traditional yellow gown to symbolize her purity, waiting for her future husband.

"Hello, I am Prince Felix. I have come to collect you, Matilda."

Matilda blushed. "You look different from how I remember, Felix."

"Oh, we were only children then," Said Marquise with a laugh.

"Come in, come in,' She said as she motioned inside the castle.

Marquise stepped into the castle and saw the gorgeous marble floors and the stained-glass windows. There was the King. He extended his hand to him. Marquise had watched Felix enough that he knew exactly what to do. He bent down on one knee and kissed the rings of the King.

"Thank you, your majesty, for trusting me with your beautiful daughter. May this marriage bring peace throughout our nations for generations to come."

The king, pleased with Marquise's answer, grabbed his hand, and pulled him up off the ground. "May Matilda bring you many sons to help you rule your land," Said the King in a booming voice.

Marquise turned to the Princess and extended his arm. "Shall we be on our way?"

She nodded and carried a few of her belongings. Marquise took those things from her, so she didn't have to carry anything. They walked down the steps of the castle on this white horse. He helped her on, and she gave one last wave to her Father, and they were off.

She wrapped her arms around Marquise's waist. "Oh, Felix, I can't wait to know you better. I have waited my whole life for you to come for me."

Marquise shivered. This is what he had always wanted. To be Felix. "We don't have to wait, you know."

MARQUISE: PART 2

"We are married, you know," Said Marquise as he took his forefinger and thumb and ran them over his moustache.

"Felix, you are so daring," Said Matilda as she twisted her hair around her fingers.

Marquise patted the horse to stop and jumped off. He helped Meredith off the horse and sat down underneath a large tree.

"Oh, I have been waiting for this day my whole life," She said as she brought a hand to Marquise's face.

"As have I," He said as he took off his shirt.

"You and I shall be the best King and Queen Utuk has ever seen," He said as he bent down to kiss Matilda.

"I vow to be your Queen forevermore," She said.

"Let's not waste this by talking," Said Marquise as he removed his belt.

"But Felix, I want to enjoy every moment," Said Matilda

"Say that again," Said Marquise as he picked Matilda off the ground and put her body against the tree they were standing next to.

Matilda looked at Felix with confusion. "To enjoy every moment?"

Marquise shook his head. "No, say my name."

Matilda smiled and took a piece of hair behind his ear. "Oh, Felix."

———

When they had finished their journey and were about to reach the castle

Marquise knew he had to tell her but didn't know how.

"Matilda, I have something I have to tell you, " said Marquise.

"I want you to know our few days together have been the best days of my life, but you must know," but then Marquise was suddenly cut off.

Felix was on his black stallion, which was running towards them.

Marquise panicked and couldn't form his thoughts into words.

Felix jumped off his horse and motioned Marquise to halt.

"Hello, my dearest Bride, I am overjoyed at the thought of spending the rest of my life with you. I deeply apologize for not coming to collect you. Please accept this flower as an apology," He said as he bent down on one knee.

Matilda looked at Marquise and then looked back at Felix. The real Felix. She turned to Marquise and let a tear slip down her face, knowing the truth.

"Oh, Felix. I have shamed our family name and you. I failed your test. Please forgive me!" cried out Matilda.

"There was no test, my bride. What are you talking about?" Felix said he as he hugged her.

"I ruined my purity with your guardsmen," She cried.

Marquise looked at Felix and shrugged.

Felix was not amused by Marquise at all.

Felix grabbed Meredith's shoulders. "My queen, please go inside the castle and make yourself at home. I have a few affairs to attend to."

She nodded and ran inside.

Felix watched her walk inside to make sure she wouldn't be witnessing what he was about to do.

"You're not even in love with her, Felix. I know you just spent the last few days running around with the nomads," Marquise said quickly.

"She didn't deserve to be treated like that," Felix snapped.

"You have been with your pirate tramp for a month, every night I know you don't want to marry Matilda…I know you had no plans of stopping your behavior either." Marqusie said trying to defend himself.

"Meredith never has to know that. You used her Marquise. I don't know how you can sleep with yourself. I should remove your pinkies for this type of behavior," Said Felix

Marquise narrowed his eyes. "You wouldn't dare."

"I would," said Felix with angar in his eyes.

"I'll tell your father you didn't get her and I'll tell him about pirate girl, " said Marquise.

Felix screamed out in frustration.

Felix pulled Marquise off his horse and hit him with all his might in the face. Marquise didn't fight back because he knew what he had done was wrong. The Prince continued to hit Marquise in the face until blood was streaming out of his nose, and his eyes were beginning to swell shut. After Marquise was utterly defeated and lying on the ground, Felix kicked him one more time in the ribs and bent down close to his ear.

"It doesn't matter what you do, Marquise, you'll never be me," Whispered Felix

---

A few weeks went by. Life with Matilda in the castle began to fall into place. Marquise's wounds had started to heal.

Felix woke in the middle of the night and carefully crawled out of bed, then left the castle. Meredith rolled over in her blankets and noticed that Felix was gone again and let out a sigh. She sat up, walked over to the balcony, and looked out into the night sky. She had many thoughts in her mind. She was far from home and didn't have any friends here...She put on her silk robe and walked down the long halls to the guards' quarters, and there was Marquise asleep on the table with a chalice in his hand. She started to wake him then stopped herself... She walked out of the room and then came back. She watched him sleep for a moment then finally after much consideration gently shook him awake.

"Marquise," She said quietly.

Marquise fluttered his eyelids, and when he realized it was the Princess, he sat straight up.

"Can I help you with something, Princess?" he asked.

"I don't think Felix loves me, and I don't know who else to talk to," She said in a whimper.

Marquise grabbed her and held her close.

"Did you ever care about me?" She asked.

"I will admit I let my lust overtake me on the day we met, but I wish I had the opportunity to fall in love with you. You have not left my mind since then," Marquise said quietly.

"Come with me," She said as she took Marquis's hand.

She led him to one of the many spare bedrooms in the castle and sat down on the bed. Marquise sat down next to her and grabbed her hand.

"I have something to tell you," She said.

Marquise's heart raced.

She took her other hand and placed it over her stomach. "I am with child," she said quietly.

Marquise gasped. "Does Felix know?" He asked.

"No! He must not know," She said quickly.

"Why?" Asked Marquise

"You're the only person I have slept with," she said, her voice broke as a tear fell down her face.

"His heart belongs to another.. I know it does. I don't know who he goes to see at night, but I know he must be seeing someone," She said and hung her head.

Marquise grabbed her hand. "Tonight, will be the last night he spends with her," he said quickly.

"I don't even know if I care," She said quietly.

"Your child will be raised a royal. Our child will be a royal," Said Marquise

"She will be raised a royal," said Matilda quickly.

"You don't know that yet," said Marquise with a smile.

"It's a girl, and her name shall be Montgomery," She said, correcting him.

After Marquise had finished talking to Matilda, he helped her to her bed and ran to the guards' quarters. He felt a deep love for the unborn child. A love he didn't know he was capable of, and he wasn't going to let even Felix in the way of her.

He dressed himself in an all-black uniform like the ones worn by the knights of Basil, a smaller country at the border of Utuk. He awoke a few of his friends and commanded them to dress in the same fashion.

"When Felix is back and asleep during the day, we will go out and murder a few of the nomads. They are wasting the Prince's time," He said.

The men didn't argue. They thirsted for blood.

BACK AT THE CASTLE: PART 15

"Bring me another roll!' Shouted Montgomery.

I ran into the dining room with three more loaves of bread and placed them on the table.

"Anything for you, Darling?" Asked Montgomery to Carac.

He shook his head.

He couldn't even look me in the eyes when he spoke.

"Slave, go clean my mother's room," Said Montgomery as she motioned with her hand for me to leave.

I nodded and exited the room, walking to the quarters. I had a guard always following me, so I didn't try to escape. James followed me everywhere. I kept silent unless I was asked a direct question.

"So where did you go when you left?" Asked James as he wedged a fingernail between his front two teeth, trying to free whatever it was that was stuck there.

"Where would you have gone, James?" I asked in a blank tone.

"The brothel," He said in a loud giggle.

I tried not to give him the satisfaction of my reaction to his ridiculous comments and just stared at him.

I began walking to the late Queen's quarters and grabbed rags and a feather duster from the corner.

There were no windows in this room, so James sat on the outside of the door and sharpened his knife.

I looked over the late Queen Matilda's things. I didn't remember much about her. She had died shortly after giving birth to Detrix, so I was incredibly young when she passed. Her crown was placed on her bed along with one of her robes. Although I had cleaned this room many times, I tried to leave everything in the place she had left it. She had always been good to me when she didn't have to be.

I didn't know if they were dreams or memories, but I remember she used to brush my hair after she had brushed Montgomery's when I was small.

I took a rag and carefully removed the dust from the rubies on her crown, then placed them back on the bed. I then took her robe, shook out the dust, and also placed it back on the bed. Just then, I heard James yell my name, and I ran to the doorway.

When I got to the doorway, James just laughed.. "I wanted to see how fast you would come," He chuckled.

I stared at him coldly, and then I realized I had knocked the crown off the bed in my hurry. I ran over to the crown to discover that a large ruby had fallen off the crown. I panicked and grabbed the ruby and crown, trying to put them back on, but something strange caught my eye, a small key behind the ruby. I took my nail and pried it out. I put the key in my palm and turned it over. It had a small "2" carved into the handle.

"What could this go to?" I thought to myself.

I put the ruby back in the crown and placed it on the bed.

I frantically searched the room, my curiosity driving me to find what the queen had hidden. I tore open her wardrobe, and it was filled with beautiful gowns in every color imaginable. I pushed the gowns aside, and there it was the only place I had never looked in the room, a tiny wooden box with a lock on top.

It was in that moment that James walked in, "What are you doing in there?"

"The queen wanted me to air out her Mother's dresses," I said quickly.

I took one of the gowns out, frantically shook it, and smiled nervously at James.

James watched me for a moment and then walked out of the room and sat back down.

I dove back into the wardrobe and pulled out the box. It was covered in dust, so I blew it off. I put the key in and heard a "clink." The lid opened, and three letters were inside. One was addressed to Felix, one was addressed to Marquise, and one was addressed to me. I put the box and the letters on the bed and slowly picked up mine. I looked over my name. This had to be from Queen Matilda.

"Why would she have written me a letter?" I thought the castle didn't like the slaves to be able to read. "And why had she written Marquise?"

That didn't make any sense either.. And what was in the letter to Felix, it was her dying wish for him to know. The letters were sealed… So, he had never opened it.. The thought seemed tragic that he would never read that one. So I chose it to open first.

I, in the moment, carefully broke the red seal on the letter to Felix,

My Dearest Husband,

I hope this letter finds you well. Over the years, you have become my dearest friend, and I am so thankful you are my husband. My health is declining. I feel myself becoming weaker every day I wake. Before I take the next step in this journey, I must share something with you while I still can. Detrix, although I love him deeply, he won't be able to stand by your side and rule the land. I watch our daughters play every day. I wish desperately that Lilith were ours. I wish that I could have given her to you. She has the heart to rule. I know, without you having to say a word, she is your daughter. She has your eyes, but most importantly, she has your heart.

Now, darling, I have one last thing to tell you. I fear for Montgomery. I don't think she has the capability of love. She doesn't care about anyone but herself. She can't follow in my footsteps. The people of Utuk will be doomed. She will doom herself as well if she is put in charge. Montgomery isn't your daughter. She is Marquise's. I know in my heart you have known all along, but I must say it now before I perish from this sickness. She was never meant to exist. It doesn't stop my love for her.. But I fear no one else can or should love her,

Please, Felix, I hope you can forgive me for keeping such a secret, but you must know. For the good of Utuk, tell your father that Lilith is yours. She is meant to be the queen.

Love, Matilda

———

My hands shook as I folded the letter back into its envelope. I had a reason to live. I had to tell Luca and the Knights. I had to tell the whole Kingdom..

I quickly put the letters into my dress and slipped the key under the bed.

FELIX: PART 1

Prince Felix jumped off his black stallion and ran to the Nomads. This was the place he felt most at home. He was greeted by small children latching on to his legs and grandmothers asking if he had enough to eat. He felt a bit guilty that they were always taking care of him. He was the Prince of Utuk after all.

There was Piper. His best comrade. They grasp hands. "I've missed you around her, brother," Said Piper.

"You know how it is. My father has a very tight grasp on me. If you know what I mean." Said Felix as hr motioned to Marquise standing behind him.

"Where is she?" Felix asked excitedly.

Piper motioned to one of the tents. Felix ran to the tents and opened the flap. There she was. She was gorgeous. Her skin was dark, and she had curly hair that touched the middle of her back. Her body was thin and lean.

She was making a basket when she turned and looked up to see who had entered the room; a smile spread across her face.

"Felix!" She exclaimed. She ran to him and jumped into his arms.

Felix catches her and holds her tight. He takes in her smell. She smelled sweet like the flowers that grew in the nomads' camp.

"Where have you been?" She asked.

"It's hard to get away from my father, you know that, and it's only been 3 days," He said as he sat her down.

"I can't wait till we can live together, and our visits can last forever," She said.

Felix grabbed one of her curls and wrapped it around his fingers, "One day, my Queen," He said softly.

"You are safer here with the Nomads until then.. I wish I were here with you instead of the castle anyway," He sighed.

"When I am King over the land, Utuk will be a place of love.. The castle will be brimming with flowers, and the children from the land can play in the gardens," He said.

Just then, Marquise walked into the tent. Felix instinctively put himself between Marquise and Cora.

"What do you want?" Felix yelled.

"I just came to remind you that the king wanted us back by dinner," Said Marquise

"I haven't forgotten," Sighed Felix.

Marquise left the tent. Felix watched him slowly walk out and then turned back to Cora.

"Felix, before you leave. I have good news. You're going to be a father," Cora blurted out quickly.

Felix stopped and stared like he didn't understand what she had just said.

"I'm with child," Said Cora loudly.

Felix stopped and smiled. "I hope they look like you," he said as he kissed her, then fell to his knees and kissed her stomach, before standing back up.

"By the time our child arrives, we will both be living in the castle together," Said Felix

"I'm going to miss all the friends I made here," Cora said as she hung her head.

"Oh, don't you worry about that. When I am king, the Nomads will live in the castle with us," Said Felix as he took her chin in his hand.

Felix knew Marquise would be interrupting them again soon, so he kissed her. "Cora, I must go right now, but I will try my best to come back tomorrow.. I will hopefully be here without…You know who and motioned to the door."

Cora smiled. "I love you, Felix."

Felix smiled back. "I love you forever." Then he left and walked back to his stallion and Marquise.

Marquise wasn't pleased. "Felix, when are you going to tell her you're married to another?"

"I haven't seen her since I was a small child. The marriage was arranged, and it isn't final until we consummate it, " He huffed.

"Your father will never allow you to marry the whore you picked up off the pirates," Spat out Marquise.

Felix looked at Marquise. "She is so much more than that, and you know it."

Marquise shrugged.

Felix was turning red with anger and took a deep breath. Then he pulled his crown out of his satchel and placed it on his head. They were getting closer to the castle.

When they reached the castle, they put their horses in the stable and began walking to the front door.

Felix grabbed Marquise's arm and pulled his ear close to his mouth. If you whisper a word of my encounters to my Father, I will pick a new head guard.

Marquise grew scared. "You can't do that," He said.

Felix smiled. "Oh, but I can, and I will if you don't allow me my freedom."

Marquise pulled his arm away and continued to walk up the steps.

The king was waiting for his son, arms crossed, when they walked in. "Felix, where have you been?" Asked the King

Felix calmly fixed his crown. "Dear father, I was busy exploring the borders of our Kingdom and making sure the Nomads hadn't wandered through the cracks again," He said happily.

The king uncrossed his arms and looked at Marquise in question.

"It's true," He said.

The king was happy with their answer and slowly walked out of the room.

"You can't hide Cora forever," Said Marquise

"When the time comes, I'm going to tell my Father," Said Felix

Marquise watched Felix run his fingers through his hair in frustration. He wondered what it would feel like to reach out and…

Felix took off his crown, placed it on the table, and picked up a bottle of wine. "I'm going to the Balcony, don't follow me," He said as he walked away.

Marquise sat still for a moment and then slowly crept up to the crown. He picked it up and placed it on his head. It felt cool on his skin. He walked over to the mirror and looked at his reflection. He saw one of Felix's robes hanging on the corner of the mirror and put that on as well. He took a deep breath and puffed out his chest. He took his hair and pulled it down into his eyes, just like Felix did.

Just then, Felix walked back into the room. Marquise quickly began taking the Prince's things off.

"What are you doing?" Asked Felix

Marquise began talking, but everything came out as a stutter.

Felix just shook his head. "Go to your quarters for the night,

Marquise." Then he picked up his robe and crown and carried them back to his balcony

FELIX: PART 2

9 months later

Felix stood on his balcony watching the stars shine when he saw Piper running to the castle. He quickly realized something was off. He knew Piper wouldn't have come unless there was a problem.

"An assassin, an assassin," Screamed Piper.

Felix ran down the steps. "What are you talking about?" yelled out the prince.

Piper was out of breath when he finally reached Felix "An assassin came through our village...He killed..So many..."

Before Piper could finish, Felix was running to the stables for his stallion. He jumped on the horse and began galloping to the nomads camp. His heart raced in fear.

When he reached the camp, he knew he was too late. Instead of being greeted by children, he was welcomed by moans of misery. Blood covered the camp. The few that the assassins hadn't slashed were holding the ones that had been. Felix ripped off his robe and a flail on his side and began making bandages from it. Then he looked up and saw her, His love, Cora, holding a baby.

He ran to her. She fell into his arms. Felix, there were many men. Dressed in all black. Her voice was soft, and it was hard for Felix to hear, so he bent down close to her lips.

"Whose Baby is this?" Asked Felix.

"This is our baby," She said as she looked down and smiled. "She came yesterday."

Felix, almost forgetting what had happened, looked down at his child. "She looks just like you," he said and then looked back at Cora, but she had fallen asleep.

Felix tied the baby to his back with the pieces of his robe and began shaking Cora. "Wake up, wake up," He screamed.

Then an older woman came up to Felix and grabbed his large

arms. "Felix, she is gone."

Felix stopped what he was doing. It was then he noticed the slashes on her legs and arms. He let out a scream that could heard across the Kingdom.

He grabbed Cora's body and cried. "Cora, I am so sorry," He yelled out.

The older woman took his face in her hands. "Felix, you did everything you could. You didn't do this to her. Those awful men did"

"Who were they? Did you recognize them?" Asked Felix

"They were the knights of Basil dressed in their black uniforms," Said the woman.

Felix carried Cora's body back to the tent where she slept. He wiped the tears from his face and turned back to the older woman. "I will be back for her. Can you keep her safe for me?"

The woman nodded, and Felix ran to his horse. Cora's blood was still on his hands when he reached the castle. He went to the guard's castle and beat on the door until Marquise answered.

"Ready the men. We are going to kill every one of Basil's guards." Said Felix

Marquise smiled. "Yes, Felix."

The Prince and guardsmen like thunder bounded into the Knights of Basil. They killed them all except one. It was a small village, but it rained blood.

The Prince looked at what the men had accomplished and saw one man standing alone.

"How does it feel to be the last knight of Basil?" Asked the Prince.

The knight stood still and raised his palm in a sign of peace.

"Grab him and bring him to me," Said the Prince.

Marquise tied the man's hands behind his back and brought him to Felix.

Felix looked down at him from his horse. "What's your name?"

"Wilburn," said the man.

"Okay, Wilbur, you will be my slave now," Said the King as he walked away.

The next day at sunrise, Felix and the Nomads gathered and buried the victims of the massacre. They held a ceremony of remembrance and played songs in tribute to the deceased.

Felix, carrying his baby, sat down a little way from everyone else and looked his child in the eyes.

Piper sat down next to him and put his arm around his friend. "Can I hold her?" He asked.

The baby began to cry... "She's hungry," said Piper.

Felix nodded... "I think I know who could take her," He said as he picked the baby back up.

Felix carried the baby back to his castle. Upon reaching the castle, he walked to his sleeping chambers, where Meredith was sleeping.

He watched her sleeping for a moment, sighed, and then walked in.

"Matilda," He said quietly.

She fluttered her eyelids and awoke. This was the first time he had spoken anything beyond pleasantries to her when they were alone since she had come to the castle.

"I'm sorry. I have something to tell you," He said.

But before he could finish, Meredith reached out and carefully took the baby from him. "You don't have to explain anything to me, Felix," She said quietly.

"Don't you want to know where she came from?" He asked.

"I don't," she said with a smile.

"What's her name?" She asked.

"She doesn't have one yet," He said slowly.

"Oh, well, a baby must have a name," She said quickly.

"What did her mother like?" Asked Matilda.

"She liked Lilies," Felix said as he wiped a tear from his face.

"Let's name her Lilith," Said Matilda.

2 years later

Felix smiled as he watched Meredith dance in the moonlight on the balcony.

"You look gorgeous tonight," He said.

"You are such a liar," She said as she grabbed her ever-growing stomach.

"I am as big as the cows in the barn," she exclaimed.

Felix walked over to her and pretended that he couldn't pick her up off the ground. "Yup, as big as a cow," He smiled.

"Oh, hilarious, why don't you become a Joker?" She giggled.

Felix laughed and picked her up, carrying her to their bed.

They both laid on the bed, and Felix took his hand and felt the baby move inside her stomach.

Later that night, Felix was playing with Montgomery and Lilith when the king approached.

"Son, the time has come for you to separate the children," Said the King

"They won't be separated," said Felix abruptly.

The King raised his eyebrows.. "That is the last time you will speak that way." Said the King in a hushed tone.

"I'm selling her tomorrow." Children are in high demand.

The king grasped Lilith to his chest. "You can't father"

The king stared at his son and sighed.. "She can stay under one condition."

"Anything. I just want to keep her safe." Said Felix

"She will be Princess Montgomery's servant."

BACK TO THE CASTLE: PART 16

Wilbur, Luca, and Detrix crept through the orchards outside of the castle. They were careful with each step, so they didn't make any sound. Luca motioned for Detrix to stop walking and slowly moved towards him.

"Where will Lilith be?" He asked as he pointed to the balcony of the castle.

"No telling at this point. I'm just hoping that Frog hasn't sold her yet," Whispered Wilbur.

"I think tonight we should separate and look through the castle after the guards have fallen asleep," Said Wilbur.

Detrix and Luca nodded in agreement with Wilbur's plan.

―

Marquise and Carac peered over the balcony through their looking glass.

"They are in the Orchards," Said Carac as he handed the looking glass back to Marquise.

Marquise squinted his eyes and peered through. "What do you think they are planning?" He asked.

Both men turned around and leaned up against the wall out of the sun.

Carac shrugged.

"Think hard, Carac, there are three men down there.. They are a small group. How would a small group plan an attack?"

"At night?" Asked Carac

"Exactly, so when they come scampering through the castle tonight, we will have traps set for them," Said Marquise.

"Smart man," said Carac as he nodded.

Montgomery tried slipping her underdress over her head, but it became stuck with her arms stuck up in the air.

She began yelling for me to help. "Slave!"

I walked into the room and leaned against the doorway, watching Montgomery frantically ran about the room with the garment blocking her vision. At that moment I did find a small bit of satisfaction of watching her run about the room in a frenzy.

"Lilith! Come here right now!" She yelled out in a whiny tone.

I decided I couldn't pretend I wasn't there much longer and walked over and pulled the garment off her head. Her face was red from screaming, and the little bit of hair on her head was completely frazzled.

"What took you so long?" She screamed.

"I guess I didn't hear you, my Queen," I said quickly.

I walked out of the room, my own voice still echoing in my ears *Queen*. She hadn't been the Queen and never would be. The realization sent a sharp thrill through me, and a smile of glee crept across my face. I alone carried the truth, and I doubted it would matter, who would ever believe me? My fingers itched to unfold the letter Matilda had written, the one that might change everything.

Detrix began picking apples and putting them into his own pockets.

Luca looked over and saw what he was doing. "Detrix, what are you going to do with 10 apples?" He questioned, but found the sight of Detrix's pockets full of fruit to be humorous.

"I'm going to give them to Lilith when we get her. She likes apples a lot," He said as he put another one in his bag.

Luca smiled thinking of Lilith trying to eat all ten apples he had saved, but didn't want to disencourage Detrix's giving heart, "I bet she will be hungry when we rescue her, too."

Luca turned back to Wilbur, "I don't understand HIM," and pointed to the castle.

"Carac?" Asked Wilbur.

"The other slave.. The one that took her. How could he?" Said asked accusingly.

"I don't know either," said Wilbur.

"She kind of," Wilbur mumbled and then trailed off.

"She already told me," Luca said quickly.

"You must know she had no one else," Said Wilbur.

Luca nodded… "I want him all to myself when it comes time."

Wilbur raised his eyebrows. "Done."

Carac walked into Montgomery's bedroom and shut the door behind him. He began unbuttoning his blouse.

"The morons are in the garden.. They will be captured by nightfall," He said.

Montgomery nodded and smiled with pleasure.

"My Dear Queen, I have kept my promises." Said Carac as he put his knees on the bed.

"Yes, you have," said Montgomery as she tore the covers off her body, completely revealing herself.

"I think it has come time for you to do me a favor," Carac said, pulling off his blouse.

"And what would that mean?" Asked Montgomery as he unbuckled his pants.

Carac moved himself in between her legs and bent down close to her ear. "Make me your King."

The door was closed, and I knew they weren't coming out for at least a few moments.. So, I ran to a spare bedroom and pulled her letters from my dress.

Lilith,

I hope this letter finds you well. I don't know if you'll remember me, but I loved you like a daughter. In my heart, you were. Your heart is pure with love and compassion. Montgomery isn't royalty. You are the rightful owner of the throne. You are the daughter of Felix. He loves you more than anyone in this world and always will. Montgomery's father is Felix's head guard, Marquise.

A tear fell from my face and splashed on the letter. I wished I could have told Felix I knew. I wished I could have hugged him in that moment.

You must inform the royalty of our neighboring countries. If things continue the way I think they will, you will be a servant, and they won't believe you. That is why I wrote this letter. It is in my handwriting, and the seal at the bottom is my seal. There is no other one like it in the world, and I requested to be buried with my seal stamp. Protect this letter with your life. It might be the only thing that can save it.

Love your adopted mother, Matilda.

I suddenly had hope in my heart, not only for myself, but for everyone in the Kingdom. I wasn't just going to restore what we once had, but I also wanted to make Utuk better then it was before.

Later that night

Detrix, Luca, and Wilbur made their way to the entrance of the castle.

Wilbur pulled Luca close to his mouth. Go around the castle and check that shed over there. That's where they used to keep us.

Luca nodded and headed down to the shack.

Wilbur and Detrix headed into the castle.

———

Marquise curled his moustache around his finger. He was in the slave's shed waiting.

———

Carac paced back and forth as he waited in the halls of the castle.

———

CHAPTER 30: ROYAL ENGAGMENT

"Gotcha," Said Marquise as he raised his sword to Luca's neck.

Luca drew his sword from his belt and raised his hands in surrender.

"You shouldn't have come here, boy," Said Marquise as he tied Luca's hands behind his back.

They walked to the dungeon, where they were greeted by

Wilbur, already behind bars, and Detrix, with his arms tied behind his back.

Luca looked Carac dead in the eyes. "How could you?" He yelled out.

"Hey brother, I tried to let you go the first time," Said Carac.

Luca shook his head. "How could you do it to her?"

Carac swallowed and broke eye contact.

"Don't talk to them, Carac. They will only put doubts in your head," Said Marquise.

Carac nodded and walked out of the room.

Marquise took Detrix and put him in his sleeping quarters and locked him inside the room from the outside.

With a heavy heart, Carac made his way back to Montgomery's bedroom. He honestly didn't want any more people to die or be enslaved, but he couldn't risk anyone destroying his chance at the crown.

He took some wine from the cellar and began drinking from the balcony. He fell asleep there watching the sun rise.

He awoke to Marquise shaking his shoulders. "It's time," He said quickly.

"Right now?" Asked Carac

"Are you arguing?" Asked Marquise almost laughing at his Luca's ignorance.

Carac smiled and quickly pushed himself off the ground. "No, Sir."

Marquise handed him a robe that had belonged to Felix's grandfather.

Carac beamed with Pride as he looked over the stitching in the garment. He slipped on the cloak and began slowly walking to the throne room.

There was Montgomery on her Throne, in all her glory. Her best red wig sat upon her head. She had powdered her face white and was wearing cakey red lipstick. She was holding a crown that her grandfather had worn before his death. It was golden, with a green emerald at its center.

Carac bent down at her feet and placed his hands on the ground.

"Carac, you have kept your promises to me and shown your loyalty. Now it is my turn to do a favor for you and ask you to be my King," Montgomery said.

Carac slowly stood up and raised his eyes to Montgomery.

"I accept," He said.

Montgomery placed the crown on his head. "Then let this be known as our royal engagement."

Montgomery turned to Marquise. "Gather our neighboring royals so that everyone will know of our marriage. "

Marquise nodded and smiled. He hoped this marriage would bring his daughter happiness and end her childish behavior.

I peeked through the crack of Montgomery's bedroom and watched Montgomery place the crown on Carac's head.

James looked over at me. "Get back to work, slave," He mumbled.

"Your just upset your first lover boy figured out how to trick the queen into becoming royalty and you couldn't even run away," Said James.

His words struck me as odd. "First," I asked. James didn't even know Luca existed.

"Yeah, your second one is down in the dungeon with the stablemen." He said as he scratched his head and then examined his nail, like he expected to find something.

"Oh no... I wasn't supposed to tell you that," He said slowly and looked up at me.

My heart began to race in fear. I felt my head growing lighter, like I might fall over. "Luca was here." I muttered without caring who heard. I had to think of a way to see him. Then my heart raced from excitement "Wilbur is alive?" I asked.

"I don't believe you," I said quickly.

James huffed. "Marquise and Carac captured them, I swear."

"You are just trying to break my spirit, James. NO one could capture MY Luca and Wilbur!" I threw the back of my hand over my forehead dramatically.

"You can see with your own eyes if you don't believe me," James quickly and grabbed my arm and began marching with me to the dungeon.

I couldn't help but smile a little. I desperately wished it were under different circumstances, but I couldn't wait to see Luca and Wilbur.

The Dungeon leaked and smelled of earth. Water from the ground splashed onto my calves as we walked through the halls.

I peered through the bars and saw Luca. He was still wearing the same white shirt he had on when I last saw him, but the sleeves had been torn off, and he looked weak.

I grabbed the bars instinctively, "Luca!" I screamed.

Luca raised his head from the dirt and quickly got up and ran over to me.

"Lilith!" He reached out through the bars and grabbed my hands grasping on.

James grabbed my shoulders and began pulling me back.

"Come on, you saw him," He said as he jerked me away.

"My father is alive," Luca said quickly.

"What?" I asked puzzled.

Luca shook his head like he was clearing his mind. "Wilbur is alive. He is here in the castle."

James, angrily, grabbed my wrist and began dragging me back up to the top of the stairs.

"See, I told you," said James.

"Well, I can see you were right," I said hoping that satisfied James.

My mind raced. "Wilbur was alive! He must be in the dungeon somewhere as well. What was Luca mumbling about his father? That made absolutely no sense. How did he even know what Wilbur looked like?"

—

Carac giggling like a young boy skipped down the halls and out into the garden with pleasure.

He took the crown off his head and looked at it in his hands. He took his fingers and ran them over the jewels. They were so bright and glistened in the sun.

He thought about how he would be treated:

When he walked down the street, people would turn their eyes in fear. They would bow down and do as he said.

He chuckled to himself at the thought. Once he started, his laughter became louder, and he couldn't control it. He fell to his knees in the garden and didn't notice when the thorns from the roses scratched down his legs and brought red blood to the surface. He clutched the crown to his chest as tears of joy fell from his eyes.

CHAPTER 31: ROYAL WEDDING

The guards began telling the women of the brothel that the Queen was planning a royal wedding, and the word spread like wildfire throughout the kingdom. Soon, people from all over Utuk were waiting outside the castle's walls to get a glimpse of the new King.

I peered out the window and looked out into the gardens. I saw people from all over the Kingdom gathering.

James peered out the window next to me "I guess they all think

Carac is going to be their savior or something."

"Yeah, I guess so," I said as I went back to scrubbing the floor of the throne room.

James sighed and sat down on the floor, "Carac is one lucky man."

"I don't know how he managed it," I said.

"Oh, I'll tell you what he did.. He climbed right into bed with the Queen and does whatever she wants…She commends his every action.. If I were only him.. I dream that Montgomery will commend me around like she does him," said James.

"Are you saying you wish you were the Prince?" I asked needing clarification.

"No, I don't want to oversee all those people and answer to the council for my actions, " he said.

I was intrigued.

"So, you just want Montgomery?" I asked.

"It's all I have ever wanted. The way she indulges herself in every aspect is so sexy." He lustfully looked in the direction of her bedroom in a daydream like state hoping to see a glimpse of her.

—

Montgomery looked over the gown she was going to wearing

for her wedding. It was crimson and white with yellow stitching sewn into the skirt.

Carac walked into her room, holding a bottle of wine, with her tiaras crooked on his head.

"Hello, my... Beloved," He said as he tripped over the gowns thrown all over the room.

"I don't have anything to wear," She said dramatically.

Carac, very drunk, exclaimed, "You're the Queen. Don't wear anything at all."

Montgomery turned to the mirror and looked at herself, smiling. "I am perfect." She said as she ran her hands on her sides.

Montgomery picked up the white dress that had previously been too small for her bust and ripped the skirt off the bottom. She examined it and pulled it over her hips and onto her waist.

She then picked up her longest black wig placed it on her head and then laid the hair on her chest. Then she put on every necklace that she owned, with only her jewels covering her chest. She finally placed her heaviest most jeweled crown on top of her head completing the look.

"This is it," she said, admiring herself.

While Montgomery was staring into her reflection, Carac sat down in front of her and began kissing her feet and making his way up her knees.

Montgomery let out a moan in satisfaction.

—

Ebba and her knights began descending into the castle gardens.

—

Montgomery entered the throne room where I was scrubbing the floors. She motioned for James to leave. He slowly walked out of the room and kept his eyes down.

"I beat you Lilith," Montgomery said excitedly.

I stopped scrubbing and continued looking at the floor. "You have always won Montgomery," I said quietly.

"I took him from you," Said Montgomery.

"Carac?" I asked.

"Don't play stupid with me," she snapped.

"I am going to sell you to the brothel along with your companion tomorrow, and the stablemen is no use to me. I shall hang him after my wedding for entertainment," She said.

I suddenly felt nauseous. I had to get to the council before Frog did anything rash. My time was quickly running out.

"I don't believe that Carac would marry a nasty Frog," I said as I made eye contact with her.

She ran over and smacked me across the face. "I'll make you watch the wedding then."

And then walked out of the room.

It was then I knew I had achieved my plan; When I was dragged into the wedding, I would yell out to the council that I had a letter for them. I could then show it to them the letter from Matilda.

The next day, everyone was busy preparing for the wedding bright and early.

Montgomery had decided to have the wedding in the throne room. So, she could be seated for the ceremony.

Marquise and the guardsmen had laid tables and chairs so that the council could spectate at the wedding.

Carac had polished the crowns and chandeliers.

Montgomery had been finishing her final look all afternoon. It mainly consisted of jewels, diamonds, and other jems.

The guards entered the room and took their positions around the throne, preparing for Montgomery and Carac's ceremony.

James had been tasked with watching me during the wedding.

He had tied my hands behind my back so I couldn't run away.

"Looks nice in here," I said.

"Yeah, it does," he said begrudgingly.

A strange side of me wanted to tell James what I was about to do, but I decided that would be foolish, and he might take my letter.

He then took a gag from his pocket and began tying it around my mouth. "Wait! What are you doing?" I asked.

I wouldn't be able to speak to the council if a gag were in my mouth.

"Sorry, Queen's orders," He said and shrugged as he tied the gag.

My heart sank, and I felt a sense of hopelessness. One of the guards began playing the harp. His hands looked graceful, slipping across the strings. Everyone started to chant in a sing-song voice, "Here comes the Queen, Here comes the King."

Everyone stood up. The doors opened in the back of the room, and the council members began walking one by one and sitting down at the round table in front of the thrones.

After the last council member took their seat, Carac made his grand entrance. He had a traditional green robe with purple stitching. Gold bracelets and necklaces were piled on his body. He was smiling like a madman. Carac looked around the room and then sat down on the king's throne. I didn't know if he was about to laugh or cry.

Then, I walked into Montgomery. She was wearing her largest gold crown with pink and green jewels. She wore a white skirt that was ripping on the sides, a long black wig, and a many necklaces with jewels that were hanging from it. Her eyes were painted with black and lips painted with bright red.

I tried to move my hands to break free, but the wrist strains were entirely too tight to move. Tears of sadness poured down my face. Montgomery looked at me and smiled. If only she knew why I was crying.

I suddenly heard a strange noise coming from the top of the throne room. I looked straight up and there was a saw.. cutting through the ceiling. "Who would be sawing through the ceiling," I thought to myself, and it was then a circle of wood falls from the sky and makes a loud "thud" in the center of the room. The music stopped, and everyone grew quiet. A rope came down and hit the floor. Then, a person dressed in a black robe began lowering themselves down the rope and then dropped to the floor. The person took off their hood to reveal their face.. I squinted. It was Ebba. She faced the group.

"I'm sorry to intrude on your wedding day, my queen, but you have something that belongs to me, my knights, I need them back now." Ebba straighted her robe and looked up at the queen like nothing was out of the ordinary.

Montgomery let out a cackle, but it was cut short. Like a bolt of lightning, fifteen horses barged through the stained-glass windows, shattering the rainbow of colors. The women had their chosen weapons raised.

The guards jumped up and raised their swords.

Everyone else in the room gasped in fright.

Luca, Wilbur, and Detrix walked in through the glass rubble and stood by Ebba.

Wilbur was holding Luca's sword.

It all made sense now. Seeing them next to each other with their similar stance and demeanor.. Wilbur was Luca's father.

Ebba turned to Montgomery, "Give me Lilith."

Montgomery motioned for James to give me to Ebba. James let go of my wrist, and I ran to Ebba. She removed my gag.

"Let's go quickly," she whispered to me as she removed the wrist strains from my hands.

"There is something I must do first," I said as I pulled the letter from my pocket.

The room was still eerily silent.

I rushed to the council members' table and handed the letter to the leader.

"What is this?" She asked, very puzzled as she brought a monocle to her eye.

I had to say something bold, something that would catch their attention. "I am here to claim my place at the throne."

I turned back and looked at my friends. Everyone looked confused. Except for Detrix, he was smiling. He had always wanted me to be queen. Since we were children.

The woman gasped and handed the letter to the rest of the council. They, one by one, read the letter and had similar reactions.

Montgomery grew increasingly red with anger as time passed. "What does it say?" She screamed. Not a single person answered her.

Montgomery got up from her throne and started to grab my arm, but before she could reach me, Wilbur pulled the sword from his sheath. "Don't take a step further," He whispered. She sat back down.

The last council member read the letter and placed it on the table, looking on in disbelief.

The leader walked over to Montgomery and handed her the letter. Marquise was so anxious that he ran over behind her throne and read the letter over her shoulder.

She quickly reads the words and then throws the letter down. "This could not possibly be true," She screamed.

She then slowly turns around and looks at Marquise. "Is this true?" She screamed.

Marquise let a tear slip down his face and tried to reach out to Montgomery's hand, but she pulled away.

Carac looked at Marquise's face. "What does the letter say?" He asked.

Marquise picked the letter up off the ground and handed it to him. Carac desperately looked at the letter and then handed it to Marquise again. "Please read it to me, for I cannot."

It was my turn to gasp. "You can't read?" I asked.

Carac lowered his head to the ground. "I cannot, I used to make up all those stories I read to you."

I gently pulled the letter from Marquise's remaining fingers and read it to Carac.

Tears of anger and frustration began to fall from his face. After I had finished, he smiled madly at me. "It doesn't matter, for I am the King of Utuk."

Luca made eye contact with me and cringed.

The leader of the council looked at Carac with pity. You are not the King, because only the Queen of Utuk can decide the King.

Carac looked at me and fell to his knees. "Lilith, it was always you. I never loved her. I love you. Make me King, Make me your King." He grasped my legs like a child begging for a treat.

I shook my head. I could tell he was getting desperately frantic.

"You remember when we danced in the halls and played pretend? We can do this the right way. He pointed to the rest of the room. It's always been us against them. Let us rule forever and tell our children how we rose from the dirt. It will be a story the world will never forget. Books will be written about us," He frantically spoke.

Luca began marching towards Carac, his eyes filled with anger.

I motioned for Luca to stop.

I pulled Carac off the ground and wrapped my arms tightly around him, because I knew it would be the last time.

After we pulled away, I looked him in the eyes and gently removed the crown from his head. "You can't do that! You can't do that!" He repeated.

"I have to Carac," I said slowly.

I placed the crown on the table in front of the council.

I then looked to Montgomery. "Get away from me, slave," she screamed out and lunged.

The council leader turned to the guards,"Withstrain her".

The guards looked at each other, confused, and then began holding Montgomery down by her arms and legs… All except

James.

"Get off of me, you animals," She yelled out.

I walked over to Montgomery slowly. I looked her in the eyes and slowly began taking the crown off her head. She tried to spit on me, but one of the guards put a gag in her mouth. The same gag I was wearing moments before.

I placed the crown on the table in front of me.

Carac grabbed my arm. "Please," he begged.

"Go back to the family you always talked about you're free," I said.

"I don't have a family!" He screeched.

He quickly jumped up and grabbed a crown from the table. "I am the King!" He yelled out.

He ran around the room with the guards chasing him. He then ran up the spiral staircase that led to a balcony high in the air that overlooked the Kingdom. He jumped up on the edge. The guards had him surrounded. He turned back and looked down at the ground far below him. He turned to everyone. "I am the King of Utuk!" he screamed. He then let out a maddening laugh and jumped off.

Everyone grew quiet again. One of the guards ran to the edge of the balcony and looked over. He turned back to the crowd and put a fist in the air.

I felt a gut-wrenching pain, but I couldn't have made him King. Luca ran over to me and threw his arms around me. "I'm sorry," He whispered. I squeezed him tight and let a tear slip down my cheek. I then let him go and quickly picked up the remaining crown, handing it to the leader.

"Crown me," I commended.

The woman smiled at me, "Yes, My Queen".

The woman placed the chunky jeweled object on my head. It felt heavy, but my heart felt free.

I looked at the knights. "Go into the cabinets of the castle and begin handing out bags of grain to the people."

Ebba nodded and walked out through the broken windows. Her knights followed close behind.

Detrix grabbed my hand. "I always knew you were my sister," He said with a smile.

Luca turned and looked at Wilbur. "Did you know?"

Wilbur smiled. "In a way, I guess I did."

The leader turned to me. "My Queen, what would you like to happen to Montgomery?"

I looked over at Montgomery, struggling underneath the guards' grip.

"Take the gag off of her," I commanded.

The knights did so. Montgomery was silent for the first time in her life. I could tell she was trembling with fear. I let her shake for a moment before I spoke.

I choose my words carefully "Montgomery, you... You have been the leech on this country."

Just the Marquise drew his sword from his belt and held it close to my neck. "You don't deserve this," He whispered in my ear.

He slowly took the blade across my neck and brought a drop of blood to the surface.

"I will die before I let you take everything from my daughter." He drew the blade back to tear my throat, and then I felt him suddenly let go and fall to the ground.

I look down at Marquise, and he has a large dart in the center of his chest.

I look across the room, and Luca is smiling with a dart gun close to his lips.

"Thank you," I mouthed to him.

Marquise reached out in his time of dying to the one he loved the best.... Montgomery.

I commend the guards for letting her go. She ran to his side and grabbed his hand. "Felix is my father? correct?" She asked still in disbelief.

He reached out his other hand to her cheek. "I love you, my beautiful daughter. I love you more then anything" Then his hand fell to the ground, and there he laid in a puddle of his own blood.

Montgomery just stared at his body for a moment in disbelief.

She stood up and looked at me. "Are you going to sell me to the brothel or are you going to kill me?" She asked.

I laughed. "I don't think the brothel would have you, Frog."

I fixed my crown. "I know what you would have done to me, Montgomery.. And I will never, in a lifetime, sink to your level of shallowness. I am going to banish you from ever coming back to this Kingdom, however."

Montgomery looked at me with fear in her eyes. "It's dangerous, I'll be killed by pirates or worse out there. You might as well hang me now. At least I would die in my own home."

"You'll have protection," I said calmly.

She looked at me, confused.

"James," I called.

He ran over to me and bowed at my feet.

"Do you vow to take care of Montgomery?" I asked.

He looked up at me and smiled with glee. "Yes, my Queen."

"Then take Montgomery to another land. If you choose to go with her, you will never be allowed to come back." I warned.

"That is a risk I am willing to take, my queen." He said quickly.

"You both have a day to leave the Utuk," I commanded.

Montgomery grabbed James's hand and they ran out of the castle, out into the gardens, through the orchards and beyond the castle gates.

Wilbur looked at me. "You should have killed them both."

"Maybe I should have, but I wanted to give them one last chance before death.. Once they are dead, they can't change their mind" I said calmly.

Luca grabbed my waist and kissed me. "I would love you forever even if you weren't the queen," He says in almost a giggle.

BACK TO THE CASTLE / THE END

One year later.

Carrot ran down the hallways of the castle, chasing a ball made by the Nomads.

Luca, dressed in a purple robe, picked up the ball from my throne and threw it again.

I walked over and sat down on his legs.

"How do you keep getting prettier?" he asked me.

I laughed. "Kissing up to the Queen, I see," I said, giving him a wink.

"So… the castle feels very lonely," I said slowly.

"Detrix and Wilbur keep you company," he replied quickly.

"While that is true… we are missing someone here," I said as I ran my fingers along his cheek.

"I took a vow to protect the people," he reminds me as if I wasn't well aware.

"I know you did… but I think you'll be more help in the castle with me," I told him.

"I don't know how to explain it to my mothers," he said reluctantly.

"You don't have to, because I already did," I replied.

He jumped up and grabbed me in his arms. "What did they say?" he asked.

"They said if you wanted to be my King, they would approve," I said.

I picked up the crown that had been sitting in the corner of the throne and placed it on his head.

"Be my King?" I asked.

Luca smiled. "Always."

THE REIGN OF LILITH (COMING SOON)

James stroked Montgomery's long hair with a pinecone, brushing all the tangles free. Her natural brown color was growing back through. She looked at her slender body in the reflection of the water.

"How much do you think the jewels are worth?" she asked.

"Enough for what we need," replied James.

"The pirates won't charge us much anyway. They enjoy killing," he said while contining to brush Montgomery's hair.

ABOUT THE AUTHOR

Lily Boone

Lily Boone lives in Louisville, Kentucky, where she finds inspiration in the city's blend of history, culture, and charm. A lifelong storyteller, she writes with a passion for weaving vivid characters and rich historical detail into captivating narratives. When she's not writing, Lily enjoys swimming, spending time with her husband, exploring new coffee shops, and going on adventures with her pug. Her work has been featured in The Literary Journal for Kentucky Community and Technical College and The Winchester Sun.

Printed in Dunstable, United Kingdom